"Aw, Lace, don't cry."

"I told you, I must have gotten something in my—" The next thing she knew, she was toppling into Noah's arms.

Noah didn't think about what he was doing, because what he was doing felt as natural as flying. Wrapping his arms around Lacey, he tilted his chin to make room for her head and widened his stance to make room for her feet between his. It wasn't the vibration of flight he sensed, but her trembling.

He kissed her. It was demanding and rousing, and once it started, it was too late to ask what she was doing back in Orchard Hill, too late to ask her anything, or to do anything but pull her even closer...

Dear Reader,

Three of my favorite occasions are weddings, a new baby's arrival and Christmas. My latest book, *A Bride Before Dawn*, contains all three. I'm a planner by nature, and yet one of the things I love most about these celebrations is their sheer unpredictability. Will it rain on an outdoor wedding? Will the baby arrive early or late? Will the kids notice if I buy rolls instead of make them from scratch? Maybe, yes and definitely.

In *A Bride Before Dawn*, Lacey Bell is a planner, too. At the top of her to-do list is: Resist Noah Sullivan. But when Noah and his brothers find a baby on their doorstep and ask for Lacey's much-needed help, resisting this fly-by-night test pilot is even trickier when he has a three-month old baby in his arms.

For me, one of the most meaningful aspects of special occasions is thinking of the perfect gift. My gift to you, dear reader, is Lacey and Noah's story. Good things are going to happen. (They really are.)

Sincerely,

Sandra Steffen

A Bride Before Dawn

SANDRA STEFFEN

MILLS BOON

First published in Great Britain 2012
by Mills & Boon, an imprint of Harlequin (UK) Limited.
Large Print edition 2012
Harlequin (UK) Limited,
Eton House, 18-24 Paradise Road,
Richmond, Surrey TW9 1SR

© Sandra E. Steffen 2011

ISBN: 978 0 263 23011 6

Printed and bound in Great Britain
by CPI Antony Rowe, Chippenham, Wiltshire

SANDRA STEFFEN

has always been a storyteller. She began nurturing this hidden talent by concocting adventures for her brothers and sisters, even though the boys were more interested in her ability to hit a baseball over the barn—an automatic home run. She didn't begin her pursuit of publication until she was a young wife and mother of four sons. Since her thrilling debut as a published author in 1992, more than thirty-five of her novels have graced bookshelves across the country.

This winner of a RITA® Award, a Wish Award, and a National Readers' Choice Award enjoys travelling with her husband. Usually their destinations are settings for her upcoming books. They are empty nesters these days. Who knew it could be so much fun? Please visit her at www.sandrasteffen.com

For my seven wonders of the world:
Anora, Leah, Landen, Anna,
Erin, Dalton & Brynn

Chapter One

Noah Sullivan understood airplanes the way physicists understood atoms and bakers understood bread.

He pulled back on the yoke, pushed the throttle forward and sliced through the clouds. He dived, leveled off and climbed, listening intently to the engine all the while, the control held loosely in his hands. This old Piper Cherokee was soaring like a kite at eighteen hundred feet. She had a lot of years left in her.

The same couldn't be said for all the planes he

flew. The first time he'd executed an emergency landing he'd used a closed freeway outside of Detroit. Last month he'd had to set a Cessna down on a godforsaken strip of dirt in the Texas hill country. He'd never lost a plane, though, and was considered one of the best independent test pilots in his field.

He wasn't fearless. He was relentless. He couldn't take all the credit for that, though. He never forgot that.

When he was finished putting the Piper through her paces, he headed down, out of the clouds. He followed the Chestnut River west, then banked south above the tallest church spire in Orchard Hill. Halfway between the city-limit sign and the country airstrip was Sully's Orchard. It was where Noah grew up, and where he collected his mail every month or so when he flew through.

He buzzed the orchard on his way by, as he always did when he came home, and tipped his wing when his oldest brother, Marsh, came running out the back door of the old cider house, his ball cap waving. Their mother used to say Marsh and Noah had been born looking up— Marsh to their apple trees and Noah to the sky above them. The second oldest, Reed, stepped out of the office, shading his eyes with his right hand. Tall, blond and shamelessly confident, he waved, too.

Those two deserved the credit for Noah's success, for they'd given up their futures after their parents died in an icy pileup when Noah was fifteen and their baby sister, Madeline, was twelve. Noah hadn't made it easy for them, either. Truancy when he was fifteen, speeding and curfew violations when he was sixteen, drinking long before it was legal. They never gave up on him, and helped him make his dream of flying come true. Maybe someday he would find a way to repay them.

He still enjoyed getting a rise out of them from time to time, but today he didn't subject them to any grandstanding or showing off.

He simply flashed his landing lights hello and started toward the airstrip a few miles away. He'd barely gotten turned around when a movement on the ground caught his eye.

A woman was hurrying across the wide front lawn. She was wearing a jacket and had a cumbersome-looking bag slung over each shoulder. He tipped his wing hello, but instead of looking up, she ducked.

That was odd, Noah thought. Not the snub. That he took in stride. But it was the middle of June, and too warm for a jacket of any kind.

And not even company used the Sullivans' front door.

Thirty years ago Tom Bender looked out across his ramshackle rural airstrip five miles east of Orchard Hill, Michigan, and saw his future. Today the pasture that had once been a bumpy runway, where he'd landed his first airplane, was a diamond-in-the-rough airfield operation with tarmac runways and hangars for commuter planes, helicopters, charters and hobbyists.

With the stub of a cold cigar clamped between his teeth and all that was left of a sparse comb-over swirling in the June breeze, he was waiting when Noah rolled to a stop along the edge of the runway. "How'd she do?" Tom asked as soon as Noah climbed down.

Running his hand reverently along the underside of the Piper's right wing, Noah said, "She handled like the prima donna she was destined to become."

"I'm glad to hear it. The paperwork's on the clipboard where it always is," Tom said, his attention already turning to the biplane coming in for a landing on the other runway. "As soon as you fill it out, Em will cut you a check."

With that check, Noah would make the final payment on the loan for his Airfield Operations Specialist training, a loan he'd been whittling away at for nine years. Anticipating the satisfaction he would feel when he read *Paid in*

Full on his tattered IOU, he headed toward the small block building that comprised the customer waiting area and Tom's office.

All eight chairs were empty and Tom's wife, Emma, was verifying a reservation over the phone on the other side of the counter. She waved as Noah took the clipboard from the peg behind Tom's desk and lowered himself into a cracked leather chair beside it.

He'd barely started on the checklist when the airstrip's best mechanic moseyed inside. "You aren't going to believe what I heard today, Noah," Digger Brown said before the door even closed. As tall as Noah, Digger had a good start on a hardy paunch he was in the habit of patting. "You care to guess?"

Noah shook his head without looking up. "I'm in a hurry, Dig."

"Lacey's back in town."

Noah's ears perked up and the tip of his pen came off the page. Lacey was in Orchard Hill?

For a few moments, he completely forgot what he'd been doing.

Digger was wearing a know-it-all grin when Noah looked up. "I figured that'd get your attention."

A few grades behind Noah, Lacey Bell used to walk to school with a camera around her neck and a chip on her shoulder. Back then she'd worn her dark hair short and her jeans tight. Noah had been doing his best to get kicked out of the eleventh grade, so other than the fact that the boys her age used to taunt her, he hadn't paid her a lot of attention. He'd heard a lot about her, though. Whether in bars, at air shows or loitering around watercoolers, men liked to talk. They'd said she was easy, bragging about their conquests the way they bragged about golf scores and fishing trips and cars. Noah's relationship with Lacey had taught him what liars men could be.

One night after he'd come home following his Airfield Operations Specialist training in Florida, he'd noticed her sitting on the steps that led to the apartment over the bar where she'd lived with her father. They'd talked, him at the bottom of those rickety stairs, her at the top. He'd been twenty and by the end of the night he'd been completely enamored by an eighteen-year-old girl with dark hair, a sharp mind, a smart mouth and a smile she didn't overuse. When he returned the next night, she moved down a few steps and he moved up. By the third night, they sat side by side.

She was the only girl he'd ever known who'd understood his affinity for the sky. She'd left Orchard Hill two-and-a-half years ago after the worst argument they'd ever had. Coming home hadn't been the same for Noah since.

"I wondered if you'd already heard, or if Lacey's return was news to you, too," Digger said.

"Where would I have heard that? Air-traffic control?" Noah asked, for he'd spent the past month crop dusting in Texas, and Digger knew it.

"There's no need to get huffy," Digger

groused. "Maybe you ought to pay Lacey a visit. I'll bet she could put a smile on your face. Wait, I forgot. You're just a notch on her bedpost nowadays, aren't ya?"

Ten years ago, after saying something like that, Digger would have been wearing the wrench he was carrying. Luckily for everybody, Noah had developed a little willpower over the years.

Eventually, Digger grew bored with being ignored and sauntered back outside where the guys on the grounds' crew were moving two airplanes around on the tarmac. Noah's mind wandered to the last time he'd seen Lacey, a year ago.

He'd been home to attend the air show in Battle Creek. That same weekend Lacey had been summoned from Chicago to her father's bedside after he'd suffered a massive heart attack. Noah had gone to the burial a few days later to pay his respects. Late that night, she'd answered his knock on her door and, like so many times before, they'd wound up in her bed. She'd been spitting mad in the morning, more angry with herself than at him, but mad was mad, and she'd told him the previous night had been a mistake she had no intention of repeating. She'd lit out of Orchard Hill again with little more than her camera the same day.

Now, if Digger was right, she was back in town.

Thoughts of her stayed with Noah as he finished the paperwork and pocketed the check Em Bender handed him. For a second or two he considered knocking on Lacey's door and inviting her out to celebrate with him. Then he remembered the way she'd stuck her hands on her hips and lifted her chin in defiance that morning after her father's funeral.

As tempting as seeing her again was, Noah had his pride. He didn't go where he wasn't wanted. So instead, he pointed his truck toward the family orchard that, to this day, felt like home.

* * *

The Great Lakes were said to be the breath of Michigan. As Noah crested the hill and saw row upon row of neatly pruned apple trees with their crooked branches, gnarled bark and sturdy trunks, he was reminded of all the generations of orchard growers who'd believed their trees were its soul.

He parked his dusty blue Chevy in his old spot between Marsh's shiny SUV and Reed's Mustang, and entered the large white house through the back door, the way he always did. Other than the take-out menus scattered across the countertops, the kitchen was tidy. He could hear the weather report droning from the den— Marsh's domain. Reed was most likely in his home office off the living room.

Since the den was closer, Noah stopped there first. Marsh glanced at him and held up a hand, in case Noah hadn't learned to keep quiet when the weather report was on.

Six-and-a-half years older than Noah, Marsh

had been fresh out of college when their parents were killed so tragically. It couldn't have been easy taking on the family business and a little sister who desperately needed her mother, and two younger brothers, one of whom was hell-bent on ruining his own life. Despite everything Noah had put him through, Marsh looked closer to thirty than thirty-six.

When the weatherman finally broke for a commercial, Noah pushed away from the door-way where he'd been leaning and said, "What's a guy got to do to get a hello around here?"

Marsh made no apologies as he muted the TV and got to his feet. He was on his way across the room to clasp Noah in a bear hug when a strange noise stopped him in his tracks.

Noah heard it, too. What the hell was it?

He spun out of the den, Marsh right behind him, and almost collided with Reed. "Do you hear that?" Reed asked.

As tall as the other two, but blond, Reed was always the first to ask questions and the first to reach his own conclusions. He'd been at Notre Dame when their parents died. He'd come home to Orchard Hill, too, as soon as he'd finished college. Noah owed him as much as he owed Marsh.

"It sounds like it's coming from right outside the front door," Reed said.

Marsh cranked the lock and threw open the door. He barreled through first, the other two on his heels. All three stopped short and stared down at the baby screaming at the top of his lungs on the porch.

A baby. Was on their porch.

Dressed all in blue, he had wisps of dark hair and an angry red face. He was strapped into some sort of seat with a handle, and was wailing shrilly. He kicked his feet. On one he wore a tiny blue sock. The other foot was bare. The strangest thing about him, though, was that he was alone.

Marsh, Reed and Noah had been told they were three fine specimens of the male species.

Two dark-haired and one fair, all were throwbacks to past generations of rugged Sullivan men. The infant continued to cry pitifully, obviously unimpressed.

Noah was a magician in the cockpit of an airplane. Marsh had an almost ethereal affinity for his apple trees. Reed was a wizard with business plans and checks and balances. Yet all three of them were struck dumb while the baby cried in earnest.

He was getting worked up, his little fisted hands flailing, his legs jerking, his mouth wide open. In his vehemence, he punched himself in the nose.

Just like that he quieted.

But not for long. Skewing his little face, he gave the twilight hell.

Reed was the first to recover enough to bend down and pick the baby up, seat and all. The crying abated with the jiggling motion. Suddenly, the June evening was eerily still. In the ensuing silence, all three brothers shared a look of absolute bewilderment.

"Where'd he come from?" Marsh asked quietly, as if afraid any loud noises or sudden moves might set off another round of crying.

Remembering the woman he'd seen from the air, Noah looked out across the big lawn, past the parking area that would be teeming with cars in the fall but was empty now. He peered at the stand of pine trees and a huge willow near the lane where the property dropped away. Nothing moved as far as the eye could see.

Every day about this time the orchard became more shadow than light. The apple trees were lush and green, the two-track path through the orchard neatly mowed. The shed where the parking signs were stored, along with the four-wheelers, wagons and tractors they used for hayrides every autumn, was closed up tight. Noah could see the padlock on the door from here. Everything looked exactly as it always had.

"I don't see anybody, do you?" Marsh asked quietly.

Reed and Noah shook their heads.

"Did either of you hear a car?" Reed asked.

Noah and Marsh hadn't, and neither had Reed.

"That baby sure didn't come by way of the stork," Marsh insisted.

A stray current of air stirred the grass and the new leaves in the nearby trees. The weather vane on the cider house creaked the way it always did when the wind came out of the east. Nothing looked out of place, Noah thought. The only thing out of the ordinary was the sight of the tiny baby held stiffly in Reed's big hands.

"We'd better get him inside," Noah said as he reached for two bags that hadn't been on the porch an hour ago. A sheet of paper fluttered to the floor. He picked it up and read the hand-written note.

Our precious son, Joseph Daniel Sullivan. I call him Joey. He's my life. I beg you, take good care of him until I can return for him.

He turned the paper over then showed it to his brothers.

"*Our* precious son?" Reed repeated after reading it for himself.

"*Whose* precious son?" Marsh implored, for the note wasn't signed.

The entire situation grew stranger with every passing second. What the hell was going on here? The last one to the door, Noah looked back again, slowly scanning the familiar landscape. Was someone watching? The hair on his arms stood up as if he were crop dusting dangerously close to power lines.

Who left a baby on a doorstep in this day and age? But someone had. If whoever had done it was still out there, he didn't know where.

He was looking right at her. She was almost sure of it.

Her lips quivered and her throat convulsed as she fought a rising panic. She couldn't panic. And he couldn't possibly see her. He was too far away and she was well hidden. She was wearing dark clothing, purposefully blending with the shadows beneath the trees.

A dusty pickup truck had rattled past her hiding place ten minutes ago. The driver hadn't even slowed down. He hadn't seen her and neither could the last Sullivan on the porch. Surely he wouldn't have let the others go inside if he had.

From here she couldn't even tell which brother was still outside. It was difficult to see anything in this light. A sob lodged sideways in her throat, but she pushed it down. She'd cried enough. Out of options and nearly out of time, she was doing the right thing.

She had to go, and yet she couldn't seem to move. On the verge of hyperventilating, she wished she'd have thought to bring a paper sack to breathe into so she wouldn't pass out. She couldn't pass out. She couldn't allow herself the luxury of oblivion. Instead, she waited, her muscles aching from the strain of holding so still. Her empty arms ached most of all.

When the last of the men who'd gathered on the porch finally went inside, she took several deep calming breaths. She'd done it. She'd waited as long as she could, and she'd done what she had to do.

Their baby was safe. Now she had to leave.

"Take care of him for me for now," she whispered into the vast void of deepening twilight.

Reminding herself that this arrangement wasn't permanent, and that she would return for her baby the moment she was able to, she crept out from beneath the weeping-willow tree near the road and started back toward the car parked behind a stand of pine trees half a mile away.

She'd only taken a few steps when Joey's high-pitched wails carried through the early-evening air. She paused, for she recognized that cry. It had been three hours since his last bottle. She'd tried to feed him an hour ago, but he'd been too sleepy to eat. Evidently, he was ready now. Surely it wouldn't take his father long to find his bottles and formula and feed him.

Rather than cause her to run to the house and snatch him back into her arms, Joey's cries filled her with conviction. He had a mind of his own and would put his father through the wringer tonight, but Joey would be all right. He was a survivor, her precious son.

And so was she.

In five minutes' time, life as Noah, Reed and Marsh Sullivan knew it went from orderly to pandemonium. Joey—the note said his name was Joey—was crying again. Noah and Marsh were trying to figure out how to get him out of the contraption he was buckled into. Reed, who was normally cool, calm and collected, pawed through the contents of the bags until he found feeding supplies.

When the baby was finally freed from the carrier, Noah picked him up—he couldn't believe how small he was, and hurriedly followed the others to the kitchen where Reed was already scanning the directions on a cardboard canister of powdered formula he'd found in one of the bags. Marsh unscrewed the top of a clear plastic baby bottle and turned on the faucet.

"It says to use warm water." Reed had to yell in order to be heard over the crying.

Marsh switched the faucet to hot and Reed pried the lid off the canister. "Make sure it's not too hot," Reed called when he saw steam rising from the faucet.

Marsh swore.

Noah seconded the sentiment.

The baby wasn't happy about the situation, either. He continued to wail pathetically, banging his little red face against Noah's chest.

Marsh adjusted the temperature of the water again. The instant it was warm but not hot, he filled the bottle halfway. Using the small plastic scoop that came with the canister, Reed added the powdered formula. When the top was on,

Noah grabbed the bottle and stuck the nipple in Joey's mouth. The kid didn't seem to care that Noah didn't know what he was doing. He clamped on and sucked as if he hadn't eaten all day.

Ah. Blessed silence.

They moved en masse back to the living room. Lowering himself awkwardly to the couch, Noah held the baby stiffly in one arm. All three men stared at Joey, who was making sucking sounds on the bottle. Slowly, they looked at each other, shell-shocked.

Last year had been a stellar season for the orchard. Sales had been good and the profit margin high enough to make up for the apple blight that had swept through their orchards the year before. Their sister had survived the tragic death of her childhood sweetheart and was now happily married to a man who would do anything to make her happy. The newlyweds were expecting their first child and were settling into their home near Traverse City. Noah had the money in his pocket to pay off his loan. Somewhere along the way he'd finally made peace with his anger over losing his parents when he was fifteen. All three of the Sullivan men were free for the first time in their adult lives.

Or so they'd thought.

"It says," Reed said, his laptop open on the coffee table, "that you're supposed to burp him after an ounce or two."

Burp him? Noah thought. What did that mean?

"Try sitting him up," Reed said.

Noah took the nipple out of the baby's mouth and awkwardly did as Reed suggested. A huge burp erupted. All three brothers grinned. After all, they were men and some things were just plain funny. Their good humor didn't last long, though. Dismay, disbelief and the sneaking suspicion that there was a hell of a lot more trouble ahead immediately returned.

Looking around for the baby's missing sock, Noah laid him back down in the crook of his arm and offered him more formula. As he started to drink again, Joey stared up at him as if to say, "Who in the world are you?"

Noah looked back at him the same way.

Could he really be a Sullivan? His eyes were blue-gray, like Reed's, but his hair was dark like Marsh's and Noah's.

"How old do you think he is?" Noah asked.

Reed made a few clicks on his computer. Eying the baby again, he said, "I would estimate him to be right around three months."

Although none of them were in a relationship at the present time, they did some mental math, and all three of their throats convulsed on a swallow. If Joey was indeed a Sullivan, he could *conceivably* have been any one of theirs.

The baby fell asleep before the bottle was empty. Too agitated to sit still, Noah handed him to Marsh, who was sitting the closest to him. When the child stirred, they all held their breath until his little eyelashes fluttered down again.

"I don't see how I could be his father," Marsh said so quietly he might have been thinking out loud. "I always take precautions."

"Me, too," Noah said, almost as quietly.

"Same here."

The baby hummed in his sleep. His very presence made the case of the reliability of protection a moot point.

"We're going to need a DNA test," Reed declared.

"I have a better idea," Noah said, already moving across the room toward the kitchen and escape.

"Not so fast!" Reed admonished, stopping Noah before he'd reached the arched doorway.

It rankled, but Noah figured he had it coming for all the times he'd hightailed it out of Orchard Hill in the past. "Can you guys handle the baby on your own for a little while?" he asked.

Two grown, capable, decent men cringed. It was Marsh who finally said, "We can if we have to. Where are you going?"

Noah looked Marsh in the eye first, and then Reed. "I heard Lacey's in town."

"Do you think she left Joey here?" Marsh asked.

Noah couldn't imagine it, but he'd never imagined that he and his brothers would find themselves in a situation like this, either. "I saw somebody on the front lawn when I buzzed the orchard earlier," he said. "It was a woman with bags slung over her shoulders. She was hunched over, so I couldn't see her well, but now I think she was hiding Joey under an oversize sweatshirt or poncho."

Reed got to his feet. "Was it Lacey?" he asked.

"I don't know. She was wearing a scarf or a hood or something. I couldn't even tell what color her hair was."

"Why would Lacey leave her baby that way?"

"Why would anybody?" Noah said. "I guess we'll know soon enough if it was her. I'll be back as quickly as I can."

He strode through the house, where the

television was still muted and where diapers and bottles and other baby items lay heaped on the table and countertops. Pointing his old pickup truck toward town seconds later, his mind was blank but for one thought.

If Joey was his, Lacey had some explaining to do.

Just once, Lacey Bell wanted to be on the receiving end of good luck, not bad. Was that too much to ask? Truly?

Looking around her at the clutter she was painstakingly sifting through and boxing up, she sighed. She was searching for a hidden treasure she wasn't sure existed. Her father had spoken of it on his deathbed, but he'd been delirious and, knowing her dad, he could have been referring to a fine bottle of scotch. She so wanted to believe he'd left her something of value. Once a dreamer, always a dreamer, she supposed.

She'd emptied the closet and was filling boxes

from her father's dresser when the pounding outside began. She wasn't concerned. She'd spent her formative years in this apartment and had stopped being afraid of loud noises, shattering beer bottles and things that went bump in the night a long time ago. It had been the first in a long line of conscious decisions.

Ignoring the racket, she swiped her hands across her wet cheeks and went back to work. After he'd died a year ago, she'd given her father the nicest funeral she could afford. She'd paid the property taxes with what little money was left, but she hadn't been able to bear the thought of going through all his things, knowing he would never be back. A year later, it was no easier.

He'd lived hard, her dad, but he'd been a good father in his own way. She wished she could ask him what she should do.

She filled another carton and was placing it with the others along the kitchen wall when she realized the noise wasn't coming from the alley, as she'd thought. Somebody was pounding on her door.

Being careful not to make a sound, she tiptoed closer and looked through the peephole. Her hand flew to her mouth, her heart fluttering wildly.

It was Noah.

"Lacey, open up."

She reeled backward as if he'd seen her. Gathering her wits about her, she reminded herself that unless Noah had X-ray vision he couldn't possibly know she was inside.

She caught her reflection in the mirror across the room. Her jeans were faded and there was a smudge of dirt on her cheek. She wondered when the rubber band had slipped out of her hair. Orchard Hill was a small city, so it stood to reason that she would run into Noah. Did it have to be tonight when she wasn't even remotely ready?

"I'm not leaving until I've talked to you," Noah called through the door.

"I'm busy," she said with more conviction than she felt.

"This won't take long."

Silence.

"Please, Lace?"

A shudder passed through her, for Noah Sullivan was proud and self-reliant and defiant. Saying *please* had never come easy for him.

"I'll break the damn door down if I have to."

Knowing him, he would, too. Shaking her head at Fate, she turned the dead bolt and slowly opened the door.

Noah stood on her threshold, his brown eyes hooded and half his face in shadow. He was lean and rugged and so tall she had to look up slightly to meet his gaze. The mercury light behind him cast a blue halo around his head. It was an optical illusion, for Noah Sullivan was no angel.

Before her traitorous heart could flutter up

to her throat, she swallowed audibly and said, "What do you want, Noah?"

His eyes narrowed and he said, "I want you to tell me what the hell is going on."

Chapter Two

Noah was as ruggedly handsome as ever in faded jeans and a black T-shirt. His dark hair was a little shaggy, his jaw darkened as if he hadn't had time to shave, but that wasn't what made it so difficult to face him tonight.

"Have you been crying?" he asked.

Lacey tried not to react to the concern in his voice. It was dangerous and conjured up emotions she wasn't ready to deal with. "I must have gotten something in my eye. I'm in the middle of something here. Now's not a good time." She moved as if to close the door.

He narrowed his eyes and looked at her so hard she almost believed he could have X-ray vision. "This won't take long."

"I mean it, Noah. You're going to have to come back tomorrow. Or the next day," she said, praying he didn't hear the little quaver in her voice. The backward step she took was pure self-preservation, for the man was a weakness for which she had no immunity. "I've had a lousy day and I'm not in the mood for company."

She was taking another backward step when he reached for her hand. Her senses short-circuited like a string of lights at the end of a power surge. His fingers were long, his grip slightly possessive. It brought out a familiar yearning born of loneliness, need and a great sadness.

"Aw, Lace, don't cry," he said, tugging lightly on her hand.

"I told you, I must have gotten something in

my—" The next thing she knew, she was toppling into his arms.

Noah didn't think about what he was doing, because what he was doing felt as natural as flying. Wrapping his arms around Lacey, he tilted his chin to make room for her head and widened his stance to make room for her feet between his. For once, it wasn't the vibration of flight he sensed, but her trembling. At first she held herself stiffly, but slowly the tension drained out of her. He didn't know what she'd been through since he'd last seen her, and he didn't want to guess what was at the root of her tears. In that place where instincts lived and survival reigned, he knew only that she needed something as simple and basic as a human touch.

It had been a year since he'd inhaled the scent of her shampoo, since he'd felt her warm breath against his neck or held her soft curves against the hard length of his body. He heard the rush of blood in his ears and he knew the cause.

He needed to stop this. He'd come here for a reason, a damn good one.

She sighed and lifted her head from his shoulder. Splaying her fingers wide against his chest as if to push away, she opened her eyes and looked up at him. For a moment, neither of them moved, not even to breathe.

Her eyes were luminous and her lashes were damp. Noah's heart skipped a beat then raced in double-time. Without conscious thought, he swooped down and covered her mouth with his.

He didn't know what the hell he was doing. Okay, he knew. He'd been imagining this ever since Digger told him Lacey was back in town.

He kissed her. It was demanding and rousing, and once it started, it was too late to ask what she was doing back in Orchard Hill, too late to ask her anything, or to do anything but pull her even closer and tip her head up and plunge into the heat and hunger springing to life between them.

She opened her mouth beneath his, and

clutched fistfuls of his shirt to keep from falling. He wasn't going to let her fall. Keeping one arm around her back, he moved his other hand to her waist, along her ribs, to the delicate edges of her shoulder blades. He massaged the knot at the back of her neck until she moaned. It was a low, primal sound that brought an answering one from deep inside him.

The kiss stopped and started a dozen times. Raw and savage, it tore through him until his heart was thundering and holding her wasn't enough. It was never enough.

His ears rang and his lungs burned and need coursed through his veins. He was guilty of slipping his hands beneath her shirt, guilty of succumbing to her beauty and his need. His right hand took a slow journey the way it had come, along her ribs, to the small of her back and lower. She locked herself in his embrace and buried her fingers in his hair, as guilty of wanting this as he was.

He covered her breast with his other hand, the

thin fabric of her bra the only barrier between her skin and his. He massaged and kneaded until she moaned again, her head tipping back. His eyes half-open, he made a sound, too, his gaze going to the boxes lining the room.

"You're packing," he said, easing the strap of her tank top off her right shoulder. "Where are you going?"

"It's no concern of yours."

"You leave a kid on my doorstep, it's sure as hell my concern," he said against her skin.

The censure in Noah's voice brought Lacey to her senses. Stiffening, she opened her eyes. She drew her right shoulder away from his lips and yanked herself out of his arms. Unable to get very far away without running into boxes, she had to make do with six feet of space between them.

She pulled her shirt down and pushed her strap up. Her breathing was ragged and her thoughts jumbled. Trying to get both under control wasn't easy. What an understatement.

The passion that had erupted had temporarily thrown her into her old habits, for she'd never been able to resist him.

Catching sight of her reflection in the mirror again, she pushed her hair behind her ears and took several calming breaths. From six feet away she could see Noah's vehemence returning.

"Why the hell didn't you tell me you were pregnant?" he asked.

Something crashed in Lacey's mind like a whiskey bottle hurled against the alley wall below. That was why Noah was here? Because for some unfathomable reason he believed she'd gotten pregnant? If she could have laughed, it would have been bitter.

"Are you going to answer my question or aren't you?" he demanded.

Again, she heard the censure in his voice. When other young girls were learning to say *please* and *thank you* and how to walk in heels and fit in with their peers, Lacey had been learning how to fend for herself. Eventually, she'd acquired those other skills from teachers and friends, books and television, but self-preservation was as deeply ingrained as her pride.

She may have been raised over a shabby bar, but she didn't have to accept his or anyone else's unwarranted reproach. "I want you to leave," she said. "Now."

His eyes narrowed. "What game are you playing, Lacey?"

She squared off opposite him. "I'm not playing with you anymore. I thought I made that clear a year ago."

Her statement would have carried more impact if her lips weren't still wet and swollen from his kiss, but she could tell by the way he drew his next breath that she'd scraped a nerve.

"Tell me this," he said, his hands going to his hips, too. "Did you leave Joey on our front porch tonight?"

She lifted her chin a notch, surprise momentarily rendering her speechless. Finally, she managed to say, "What do you think?"

"I *think* that if you did, it's a hell of a way to tell a man he's responsible for a kid."

It was her turn to feel stung. Obviously, he didn't know her at all. That was the problem, wasn't it? He told her what he wanted and needed and she pretended to want and need the same thing. Until two-and-a-half years ago, that is. That was when the truth had come out. It was the same night they'd broken up. It hadn't been pretty, but it had been necessary in order for her to move forward in her life, and all the other mumbo jumbo she read in self-help books.

She straightened her back and stiffened her upper lip. It rankled slightly that she had to remind herself that she'd done nothing wrong and, consequently, owed him nothing.

"If he's mine," he said, on a roll, "the least you could have done was sign the damn note so we wouldn't have to wonder which of us is his father."

She didn't know how to respond to that. Noah made her head spin. He always had.

She'd fallen in love with him when she was eighteen years old. By the time she'd realized that he'd needed his lofty dreams of freedom more than he'd needed her, it had been too late to guard her heart from getting broken every time he flew off into the wild blue yonder. Eventually, she'd found the courage to chase her own dream.

Now here she was, back where she'd started. No matter what Noah thought, she wasn't the same girl she'd been ten years ago, or five, or even one. Now she had to think about what she needed.

She walked to the door and held it open. "I asked you to leave."

"Are you going to answer my question?" he asked roughly, squaring off opposite her in the doorway.

Gathering her dignity about her, she said, "A baby. That would be the ultimate tether, wouldn't it? What would you do if I said yes? Would you marry me, Noah?"

A slap wouldn't have stunned him more.

"That's what I thought," she said, unable to close the door while his foot was in it.

Tires screeched and a horn honked out on the street. The fracas seemed to bring him to some sort of decision. Staring into her eyes as if he could see all the way to her soul, he said, "Dinner is at one at the homestead tomorrow. Be there."

The deep cadence of his voice hung in the air for a long time after he left. Lacey closed the door, but she moved around the cluttered apartment as if in a trance.

Noah Sullivan had a lot of nerve. It was just like him to threaten to break her door down if she didn't let him in and then trounce off as if everything that had happened was her fault. He made her so mad.

She closed her eyes, because that wasn't all she felt for him. She'd gone an entire year without seeing him, without talking to him or touching him, and then, bam, she'd spent one minute in his presence and wound up in his arms. Why did her body always seem to betray her when it came to Noah?

She knew the answer, and it had as much to do with love as it did with passion. She stomped her foot at the futility of it all.

From what she could gather from the little he'd told her tonight, somebody had left a baby on the Sullivans' doorstep. It wasn't clear to her why Marsh, Reed and Noah were uncertain which of them was the father. The entire situation seemed ludicrous, but if Noah believed the child might have been a product of their night of passion last year, the baby must be an infant.

What kind of a mother left her child that way?

A desperate one, Lacey thought as she looked around the old apartment where she'd spent her formative years. She understood desperation.

Shortly after her father died last year, the company she'd worked for in Chicago had downsized and she'd found herself unemployed. Her meager savings had quickly run out. Part-time and temp jobs barely put food on the table. Before long she was behind on her rent. And then things got worse.

She placed a hand over the scar on her abdomen, then just as quickly took her hand away.

She didn't have time to feel sorry for herself. She couldn't change the past, and who knew what the future held?

Right now, what she needed was a viable means of support. What she had—all she had—was this narrow building that housed her father's boarded-up bar and this ramshackle apartment above it. Although she'd promised herself that she would never move back to Orchard Hill, the deed to this property gave her a handful of options she wouldn't have had otherwise. She could reopen the bar, or rent out the building and this apartment, or sell it all—lock, stock and barrel.

As she returned to her packing, she thought

about Noah's invitation. Okay, it had sounded more like an order. Dinner was at one tomorrow, he'd said. He expected her to be there.

She wondered what he would do when she didn't show up. She spent far too much time imagining what would happen if she did.

There were two types of guys. Those who asked permission. And those who begged forgiveness. Why, Noah wondered, did he always land in the latter category?

He'd had every intention of knocking on Lacey's door and asking her one simple question. "Is Joey my son?"

But he'd seen her tears, and he'd reached for her hand, and one thing had led to another. Now here he was, pulling into his own driveway, the remnants of unspent desire congealing in his bloodstream while guilt fought for equal space. Since there wasn't much he could do about his failings right now, he pulled his keys from the ignition, turned off his headlights and got out.

The house was lit up like a church. Even the attic light was on. The windows were open, but other than the bullfrogs croaking from a distant pond and a car driving by, he didn't hear anything. He hoped that was a good sign.

He went inside quietly, and found Marsh and Reed in the living room again. They were standing in the center of the room, staring down into the old wooden cradle between them. There was a streak of dirt on Marsh's white T-shirt and Reed's hair was sticking up as if he'd raked his fingers through it. Repeatedly.

Noah waited until they looked at him to mouth, "How long has he been sleeping?"

After glancing at his watch, Marsh mouthed back, "Four minutes."

"Did you talk to Lacey?" Reed whispered.

Noah nodded and tried not to grimace.

As if by unspoken agreement, they moved the discussion to the kitchen. Keeping his voice down once they were all assembled there, Noah said, "Lacey didn't leave Joey on our doorstep."

"She told you that?" Reed asked.

"She didn't have to. If I hadn't been in shock, I would have realized it right away. If she'd been pregnant with my kid, she would have gotten in my face or served me with papers. She wouldn't have left the baby on my porch and then crept away without telling me."

"You're positive?" Reed asked.

"Covert moves aren't her style," he said. "If Joey is a Sullivan, he isn't mine."

Marsh, Reed and Noah had personalities very different from one another. But one thing they had in common was an innate aversion to asking permission to do what they thought was best. Consequently, Noah wasn't the only member of this family who sometimes wound up in the uncomfortable position of asking for forgiveness. Remembering all the times these two had been waiting for him when he'd broken curfew or worse, and all the times they must have wondered what the hell they were going to do with him, he felt an enormous welling of affection for his brothers.

"Obviously, you were both with somebody a year ago. Do either of you have an address or phone number?" he asked.

The first to shake his head, Reed was also the first to drag out a chair and sit down. "She was a waitress I met when I was in Dallas last summer. She spilled salsa in my lap and was so flustered she tried to clean it up. I stopped her before— Anyway, she blushed adorably and said her shift was almost over. She had a nice smile, big hair and—" His voice trailed away.

"What was her name?" Marsh asked after he'd taken a seat, too.

In a voice so quiet it wasn't easy to hear, Reed said, "Cookie."

Noah didn't mean to grin. Marsh probably didn't, either. It was just that the fastidious middle Sullivan brother normally went out with women named Katherine or Margaret or Elizabeth.

"What's her last name?" Noah asked.

"I've been trying to remember ever since we brought Joey inside."

Reed Sullivan had sandy-blond hair, but his whisker stubble was as dark as Noah's and Marsh's. Letting whisker stubble accumulate was a rare occurrence, so rare in fact that Noah had forgotten how dark it was. Scratching his uncommonly stubbly cheek, Reed looked beyond mortified. If he expected chastisement, he wasn't going to get it from either of his brothers.

"You said she was a waitress," Noah said, trying to make a little sense of a very strange situation. "What was the name of the restaurant?"

Reed said, "It was a small Mexican place near the airport. Now I wish I'd used a credit card so there would be a paper trail."

Noah turned his attention to Marsh, who had grown unusually quiet. "What about you? Are you dealing with a one-night stand, too?"

Marsh shook his head. "Her name is Julia Monroe. At least that's what she told me." His voice got husky and took on a dreamy quality Noah had never heard before. "I met her on vacation last year on Roanoke Island. We slept under the stars and visited just about every coffee shop up and down the Outer Banks."

"Have you talked to her since the week was over?" Reed asked, obviously as curious as Noah.

"The number she gave me was out of service," Marsh answered.

That seemed odd to Noah, but there wasn't much about this dilemma that didn't seem odd. "What about the note?" he asked. "Does the handwriting look familiar to either of you?"

Marsh and Reed wore similar expressions of uncertainty. After a moment of quiet contemplation, Reed asked, "Why wouldn't she have signed the note? Or addressed it?"

It was just one more thing about this situation that didn't make sense. Leaning back in his chair, Noah thought about the note. It hinted at desperation, contained a written plea and a promise that Joey's mother would return for him. Maybe that was all she wanted them to know.

"Does the middle name *Daniel* mean anything to either of you?" Noah asked.

Again, Marsh and Reed shook their heads.

Reed said, "We're back to square one. We're going to need a DNA test. I checked online a little while ago. Kits are available at drugstores everywhere. The test looks pretty straightforward and simple to perform, but it can take up to six weeks to get the results."

"I don't want to wait six weeks," Marsh said firmly.

"Neither do I," Reed said with the same amount of force. "Our only alternative is to hire a private investigator."

Reed reached across the table for his laptop. Marsh went to the cupboard and dragged out an old phone book.

Before either of them went a step further, Noah stopped them. "You can't pluck some name off the internet or from the phone book for something this important."

"Do you have a better idea?" Reed asked.

As a matter of fact, Noah did. For once in their lives, having a hellion for a brother was going to come in handy. "A few years ago I tested an airplane for a guy calling in a favor. He's a P.I. over in Grand Rapids and flies a blue biplane called Viper. I don't have a business card but I know somebody who does. I'll make a few phone calls first thing in the morning."

"Is this investigator any good?" Marsh asked.

Noah said, "He's found runaways and exes and bail jumpers and just about everything in between."

His stomach growled audibly. Trying to remember how long it had been since he'd eaten, he went to the refrigerator and opened the door. He saw various cartons, bags and containers of leftover takeout, one of which was starting to resemble a science experiment. This was why he always cooked when he was home.

"When are you leaving?" Marsh asked.

"I'm not," Noah said, cautiously sniffing a carton before tossing it into the trash. The science experiment went in next.

"You don't have another flying engagement lined up?" Reed asked.

"It'll keep." Unlike the leftovers on the top shelf. "I'm not going anywhere until this is resolved. I figure we can use a couple of extra hands around here."

While Noah threw out everything except eggs, butter, condiments and cans of soda and beer, Marsh and Reed talked about what they might expect on Joey's first night here. According to the information Reed had gotten from the 83,000 Google hits, children this age generally required a feeding every two to six hours.

"You're saying we could be in for a long night," Noah said, closing the refrigerator.

Reed was fast at work on a preliminary

schedule. Following a little discussion, Noah was assigned the third watch.

He ate a peanut-butter sandwich standing up. After chasing it down with a cold beer, he strode to the stairway on the other side of the room. "I'm going to get some sleep. Wake me up when you need me. I mean it. We're in this together."

"Noah?" Marsh said quietly.

With one hand on the doorknob, Noah looked back at his oldest brother.

"I'm glad you're here," Marsh said.

"*Glad* barely scrapes the surface," Reed said, closing his laptop.

Something constricted deep in Noah's chest. "I'm glad to be here." It was the honest-to-God truth.

He could have left it at that, but opportunities like this didn't come along every day, so of course he cocked his head slightly and said, "Sex on the beach, and big hair and big—" He cleared his throat. "Who knew you two had it in you?"

He dodged the roll of paper towels Marsh threw at him, and took the steps two at a time. In his room at the end of the hall, he emptied his pockets of his keys and change and put the check from Tom Bender on his dresser, then quickly stripped down. Heading for the only bathroom on the second floor, he thought about the apology he owed Lacey.

He turned on the shower. While he waited for the water to get hot, he considered possible ways he might say he was sorry. Red roses, he thought as he lathered a washcloth and scrubbed the day's grime from his arms, chest and shoulders. In his mind's eye he saw a dozen red roses upside down in Lacey's trash can. A box of chocolates would meet with the same fate.

By the time he dried off, he knew what he had to do. It wasn't going to be easy.

Begging forgiveness never was.

Chapter Three

Sure, the rusty thermometer on the light pole in the alley behind Bell's Tavern registered eighty-one degrees, but the bright afternoon sunshine wasn't the only reason Ralph Jacobs was sweating.

"You're getting a bargain," Lacey said patiently as her dad's former customer placed another bill in her outstretched hand.

"Six hundred's a little steep, doncha think?" he groused, mopping his forehead with a folded handkerchief. "That old Chevy is close to twenty years old, you know."

She glanced at the pickup truck now sitting on Ralph's flatbed trailer. She could have gotten more for her dad's pickup if she'd had time to advertise, and they both knew it.

Turning her attention back to the transaction, she watched as Ralph wet his finger and reluctantly added another hundred spot to the others in her hand. "Dad always took good care of that truck," she said. "It was ten years old when he bought it. Remember how proud he was that day? It still has low mileage and started just now the first time you turned the key. You and I agreed on $600."

"It has four flat tires," he insisted.

"I threw those in at no extra charge."

Ralph made a sound she would have been hard-pressed to replicate. When he finally parted with the sixth hundred-dollar bill, she handed him the signed title and tucked the money into the pocket of her faded cutoffs for safekeeping.

Just then Lacey's best friend came hurrying

down the steps, her light brown curls bouncing and her white blouse nearly as bright as the sunshine. "It was good of you to offer to drop these boxes at Good Neighbors on your way home, Mr. Jacobs," April Avery called as she secured the last carton on the trailer with the others.

Ralph made that sound again, because it hadn't been his idea.

April was one of those savvy, quirky women nobody could say no to. She'd moved to Orchard Hill after she married into the large Avery brood seven years ago. She and Lacey had clicked the first time they met and had become the best of friends in almost no time.

Together they watched as the trailer carrying many of the things Harlan Bell could no longer use rattled away. The moment they were alone again, April pushed her curly hair behind her ears and exclaimed, "I thought he would never leave. Now, finish your story."

"Where was I?" Lacey asked. As if she didn't know.

"You were just getting to the good part," April said. "Noah threatened to break your door down if you didn't open it, and the instant you did, he took you in his arms and kissed you so thoroughly you swooned. That is so romantic."

There was never much activity in the alley at this time of the afternoon in the middle of the week. Two boys had taken a shortcut through here on their bikes a few minutes ago. A panel truck was making a delivery to the appliance store at the other end of the alley, but the deliverymen were too far away to hear Lacey say, "I did not swoon. And it wasn't romantic."

"Then your heart *didn't* race and your knees *didn't* weaken and butterflies *didn't* flutter their naughty little wings in unmentionable places?" April asked.

Lacey held up a hand in a halting gesture. Just thinking about Noah's kiss was stirring up those butterflies again.

"That's what I thought," April said, nudging her with one shoulder. "You're lucky. The only romance I've had since Jay's been deployed is via webcam. Trust me, it's not the same as real kissing."

Lacey stared at her friend. "You and Jay have webcam sex?"

"Never until after the twins are in bed, but we're talking about you."

Smiling at April's one-of-a-kind sense of humor, Lacey wandered to the metal trash can lying on its side under the stairway. She set the can upright and put the lid on with a loud clank. Next, she unlocked the tavern's back door and the two of them went inside.

April's in-laws owned the busiest realty company in Orchard Hill. She'd been working in the office and pursuing her real estate license since her husband, a guardsman, had been called to active duty eight months ago. She was here this afternoon as Lacey's friend but also to offer her professional opinion regarding a selling strategy for the tavern. It would be her first solo listing.

While April poked her head into the empty storage room that had once housed kegs of beer and crates of liquor, Lacey went to the front door and propped that open, too. Standing in the slight cross breeze, she tried to see the place through a Realtor's eyes.

When it came to bars in Orchard Hill, Bell's Tavern had been near the bottom of the food chain. Lacey had always gotten the impression that her dad had liked it that way. Originally, the building had been a mercantile exchange. It had passed hands several times before being converted into a tavern eighty years ago. The ceilings were low, the sidewalls were exposed brick and the hardwood floors desperately needed refinishing. The tavern's most redeeming features were the old speakeasy door from Prohibition days, now leaning against the wall in the storeroom, and the ornate hand-carved mahogany bar and matching shelves behind it. The mirror had been cracked when her dad bought the place, so she couldn't blame that for her run of bad luck this past year.

She thought about the itemized hospital bill tucked inside her suitcase upstairs. Before her phone had been shut off, bill collectors had called at all hours of the day and night. The wolves were at her door.

"Do you think Avery Realty will be able to find a buyer for this place?" she asked.

"Is that really what you want?" April countered.

Sliding her hands into the pockets of her cutoffs where all the money she had to her name crinkled reassuringly, she said, "I have to sell, April."

April gave one of the barstools a good spin. "Don't mind me. I've been having serious separation issues ever since Jay left for Afghanistan. It's selfish of me, but I want you to stay. Don't worry, we'll find a buyer for this place, although in this economy it could take a little while. In the meantime, I've been thinking about the hidden treasure your dad mentioned before he died."

"I've searched everywhere," Lacey insisted, putting one of the cameras from her mother's collection back on the high shelf where she'd found it. "There's nothing here. Even this old Brownie has more sentimental value than monetary worth."

"Maybe the hidden treasure isn't a tangible object," April said. "I think that's what your father was trying to tell you."

"What do you mean?" Lacey asked.

April stopped testing every barstool and looked back at her. "You're in Orchard Hill and Noah is in Orchard Hill. Maybe the hidden treasure is the lodestar that keeps bringing you two together. You know, Fate."

"Oh, man, I hope that wasn't what he was talking about," Lacey declared. "I'm not even on speaking terms with Fate anymore."

Lacey was relieved when April let the subject

drop, because she couldn't have argued about the unreliability of Fate with someone whose husband was dodging land mines and shrapnel on the other side of the world. Leaving her friend to get the measurements she would use in the real-estate listing, Lacey took stock of her situation.

She'd taken a leap of faith when she'd moved to Chicago more than two years ago. It was never easy to start over in a new place, but she'd made a few friends there, and although her job as an administrative assistant had been mundane much of the time, it had paid the bills. She'd taken night classes and dared to believe that her future had potential.

Then her dad died and the company she'd worked for downsized and she was let go. A few months later she'd wound up in the emergency room, and what was supposed to have been a simple surgery sprouted complications. Not long after that, she'd received an eviction notice. Her last temp job had barely left her with enough money to cover the bus ticket back to Orchard Hill. She didn't know how she would ever repay the hospital unless she sold the tavern. So, no, she didn't care to place her faith in something as flighty as Fate.

When April had all the information and measurements she needed to pull some comparables and start working on a selling strategy, Lacey saw her to the front door. After promising to come by later to see April's three-year-old twin daughters, Lacey flipped the dead bolt. She was on her way to turn out the light in the storeroom when she noticed a cue stick lying on the pool table in the corner. She headed over to take care of it, the quiet slap of her flip-flops the only sound in the room.

There was a nagging in the back of her mind because she didn't recall seeing the cue stick lying out when she'd been down here yesterday. Wondering if she simply hadn't noticed, she went around to the other side of the pool table to put the stick away. She hadn't gotten far when she saw something on the floor beneath the pool table.

She bent down for a closer look and found a sleeping bag carefully tucked under the wood skirting of the pool table. Her breath caught and a shiver ran up her spine.

She might have overlooked the cue stick, but she'd swept these floors yesterday and was positive the bedroll hadn't been here then. That meant somebody had been here between last night and today.

How could anyone have gotten in? The doors and windows had been locked, the whole place battened down tight.

She searched her mind for a possible explanation. If Orchard Hill were a larger city, she might suspect that a homeless person was camping out in the empty tavern. She was more inclined to think a teenager or a college student might have done it. That didn't explain how someone could have gotten in. And since when did teenagers or college students fold things up neatly? It didn't make sense to leave the sleeping bag here.

Lacey went perfectly still. Maybe the intruder hadn't left.

Was someone here now?

Her heart raced and goose bumps scurried across her shoulders. Shattering beer bottles and loud voices didn't frighten her, but this eerie quiet had her imagination running wild.

There was a light on over the bar and another one over the pool table. The windows on the east wall faced the brick building next door, allowing very little natural light inside. Suddenly, every corner in the room seemed too dark and every doorway a potential hiding place for someone lurking menacingly in the shadows.

From behind her came a soft thud. Her hand flew to her mouth and her breath lodged in her throat.

The sound came again. It was a footstep—she was sure of it—followed by the creak of a floorboard. She spun around. And saw Noah pause just inside the back door.

"Oh! It's you," she said on a gasp.

Noah came closer, one thumb hitched in the front pocket of low-slung jeans. The fingers of his other hand were curled around the handle of an infant carrier.

His eyes were in shadow, but one corner of his mouth lifted in a humorless grin. "The door was open so I didn't knock. I didn't mean to startle you," he said. "I came here to tell you I'm sorry. I guess I should apologize for scaring the daylights out of you while I'm at it."

Prying the cue stick out of her clenched hands, she laid it on the table where she'd found it. She carefully wound her way around small tables with mismatched chairs, and arrived at the bar shortly after him. She was glad when he started talking, because she would have had a hard time getting anything past the knot in her vocal cords.

"There's someone I'd like you to meet." He

lifted the car seat a little higher so she could see the baby sleeping inside. "My nephew, Joseph Daniel Sullivan. He likes to be called Joey."

"Your *nephew?*" she managed to ask.

"You don't have to keep your voice down," Noah said. "He can sleep through anything, as long as it's his idea."

So the child already had a mind of his own. He sounded like a Sullivan, Lacey thought.

Gently, Noah placed the car seat on the bar and continued. "I had no right to accuse you of leaving Joey on our doorstep last night. It's no wonder you didn't join us for dinner today. That reminds me." He reached into a canvas bag he'd placed beside the baby, and brought out a clear, covered bowl of spaghetti. "I brought a peace offering."

The next thing she knew she was holding the bowl, still slightly warm, in her hands.

"Are you ever going to say anything, Lacey?"

She raised her chin and opened her mouth only to reverse the process. She didn't know what to say. What did a girl say when she was standing three feet away from her first love, a man who looked as if he hadn't slept, a man whose dark hair was a little too long to be considered civilized, but who continued to keep a steady hand on the car seat where an unbelievably small baby slept?

"Did you use your homemade spaghetti sauce?" she asked, only to groan aloud.

She could tell by the slight indentation in his left cheek that his grin was no longer humorless. "Would you accept my apology if I said yes?" he asked.

Lacey wasn't ready to smile. She wasn't one to get angry and get over it. For her, forgiveness was a process. "So this is Joey," she said, moving to a safer topic. "Have you determined whose son he is?"

With a shake of his head, Noah said, "We won't know for sure until Marsh and Reed have a DNA test and get the results. Meanwhile, they're hoping they can locate Joey's mother as quickly as possible, not that it's going to be easy. They're meeting with the P.I. right now. I'm on baby duty. You can ask me anything you want, but first, I'd like to finish my apology."

Lacey placed the bowl of spaghetti on the bar with her camera. Settling onto one of the stools, she made a show of getting comfortable.

Noah eased onto the stool next to her. Looking at her in the mirror, he said, "Our breakup two-and-a-half years ago came as a shock to me. Hell, it blew me out of the sky. Looking back, I realize it shouldn't have."

She wanted to tell him to stop, because this was dangerous territory, more dangerous than he knew. She took a deep breath and willed herself to hear him out.

"I don't know how I could have missed the clues," he said. "But I did. If there was a little kid within a hundred feet, your eyes were on him. Just like now."

She dragged her gaze from Joey and stared at Noah's reflection. He had the tall, rangy build of a barroom brawler. One of these days he would probably get around to shaving, but it wouldn't change that moody set of his lips or the depth in his brown eyes. He rarely talked about himself. On the surface, he was all bluster and swagger. If a woman was patient and paid attention, every once in a while she caught a glimpse of the part of him he kept hidden most of the time.

One day after she'd been seeing him for about a year, he'd taken her flying. It was during that flight that she'd learned how he felt about becoming a father. He was wonderful with kids—she'd seen that for herself—but his feelings about parenthood had nothing to do with how children responded to him and vice versa. That May morning, two thousand feet above the ground, he told her about the day his parents died in an icy pileup on the interstate.

Every now and then someone in Orchard Hill recalled a memory of Neil and Mary Beth Sullivan. Noah's mother and father had been well liked and were sadly missed. It was common knowledge that Marsh had stepped directly out of college and into the role of head of the family after they'd died, and that Reed came home two years later to help. The youngest, Madeline, had been everyone's darling, and Noah was the hell-raiser everybody worried about.

Until that day, Lacey hadn't known he'd been in the car when it crashed. With his eyes on the vast blue sky outside the cockpit and the control held loosely in his able hands, he'd described the discordant screech of tires and the deafening crunch of metal. Trapped in the back, he hadn't been able to see his parents. But he'd heard the utter stillness. The silence. Fifteen-year-old Noah had walked away with a broken arm and minor cuts and bruises—an orphan. He didn't remember much about the days immediately following the accident. During the burial, the fog in his brain had lifted and he'd solemnly vowed that he was never going to put a kid of his through that. He wasn't going to have children. Period.

Over the years she'd tried to find the words to tell him that lightning didn't strike twice and that their children wouldn't be orphaned. But who was she to make that promise?

She'd loved him, and for a long time she'd told herself what they shared was enough. He was right, though. She never had been able to keep her eyes off little ones. After April and Jay had their twins three years ago, yearning to have a baby of her own became an ache she couldn't pretend didn't exist.

"Until you spelled it out for me," he said, drawing her back to the present, "I didn't know you even *wanted* kids. But you did. And I didn't. It was a classic breakup. End of story, right?"

Lacey remembered the day she'd ended things with Noah. They used to fight sometimes. When it happened, their arguments were messy and noisy. That final night neither had raised their voices. It made their breakup unforgettable on every level.

"Then we wound up in bed last year," Noah

said. "And Joey is about the right age to have been a product of that night. That's no excuse for barging into your apartment last night and accusing you of deserting him. I hadn't seen you in a while, but I should have known. People don't change. You knew how it felt to lose your mother. *You* never would have left a baby on my doorstep. Slapping me with a lawsuit or siccing the cops on me—that I could see you doing."

Nothing else could have made her smile just then.

Their gazes met, and this time it wasn't in the mirror. Emotion swirled inside her, welling in her eyes. Her doctor in Chicago had told her that sudden tears were part of her healing process. She had a feeling it was too much to hope that Noah didn't notice.

She knew how she looked. Her fine dark hair skimmed her shoulders and turned wavy in the summer humidity. Her shorts were threadbare, her T-shirt was thin and her breasts were sensitive. No doubt he noticed that, too.

She found herself looking into his eyes again. It was easy to get lost in that dark brown gaze. There was a time when she wouldn't have been able to drag her eyes away. Last night, for example, and a hundred other nights, too.

Today she flattened her hands on the worn surface of the bar and slid off the far side of her stool. "Okay. I forgive you for scaring the daylights out of me and for accusing me of leaving Joey on your doorstep."

He stood, too. Cocking his head slightly, he said, "Can I get that in writing?"

She rolled her eyes, but she couldn't help smiling, too. Feeling lighter—perhaps there was something to this forgiveness business—she spied her favorite 35 mm camera. The instant it was in her hands, she felt back in her element. She aimed it at Joey, adjusted the focus and snapped a picture.

The poor baby jerked. His little hands flew up and his eyes popped open. Surprisingly, he didn't cry. Instead, he found her with his unwavering gaze.

His eyes were blue and his cheeks were adorably chubby. Fleetingly, she wondered how his mother could stand to be away from him for even a day.

"I'm sorry," she murmured quietly. "I didn't mean to startle you. The next time I'll ask for permission before I take your picture. Deal?"

The change in his expression began in his eyes. Like the wick of an oil lamp at the first touch of a lighted match, delight spread across his little features, tugging the corners of his lips up until his entire face shone.

"May I take another one?" she asked him.

He smiled again, this time for the camera. He was a Sullivan all right. Marsh and Reed didn't need a DNA test to determine that much.

"I can't believe it," Noah said.

She glanced up and snapped his picture, too. "What can't you believe?"

"It's the first time I've seen him smile. He obviously has good taste in women."

She wished she didn't feel so complimented.

"Would you like to hold him?" he asked.

She ached to. "Maybe some other time."

There was a moment of awkwardness between them. They weren't a couple anymore, and neither knew what to say. After a few more seconds of uncomfortable silence, Noah picked the baby carrier up by the handle, an effortless shifting of muscles and ease, and said, "I guess I should get this little guy home." He slipped the strap of the diaper bag over one shoulder then started toward the back door where he'd entered ten minutes earlier.

Lacey slid her hand inside her pocket. Reassured that her nest egg was still safe and sound, she glanced into the shadowy corners around the room. Goose bumps popped out up and down her arms all over again.

With her camera suspended from the strap around her neck, her key in one hand and the bowl of spaghetti in the other, she hurried after Noah, locking the door behind her as she left. While he wrestled to secure the car seat properly in the seat of his truck, she started up the stairs.

"Lacey?" he called when she was halfway to the top.

She glanced down at him. "Yes?"

He was looking up at her, his eyes hidden behind dark glasses. "I'm glad you're back. Orchard Hill hasn't been the same without you."

She didn't have a reply to that because she wasn't sure how she felt about being back. She climbed the remaining stairs and let herself into the apartment. After putting her camera and the spaghetti away, she stood for a moment catching her breath and willing her heart rate to settle into its rightful rhythm.

When Noah was gone, she went out again, locking that door, too. She cut through the alley and emerged onto Division Street.

Orchard Hill was a college town of nearly

25,000 residents. Three seasons of the year, the downtown was teeming with activity. Now that most of the students had gone home for the summer, Division Street had turned into a sleepy hometown main street. That didn't keep her from looking over her shoulder this afternoon.

Her first visit was to the electronics store three blocks away where she studied the wide assortment of cell phones before choosing one she could afford. Her first call an hour later on her prepaid, bare-bones cell phone was to the Orchard Hill Police Department. After all, it was one thing to be unafraid of things that went bump in the night and another thing to ignore evidence that somebody had gotten into a locked tavern and slipped out again with barely a trace.

Lacey knew how a shadow felt.

She'd waited an hour for the police cruiser to

arrive. Now she wasn't letting the man in blue out of her sight.

She'd shown Officer Pratt the sleeping bag and cue stick, and explained the situation as best she could. She answered his questions then remained an unwavering six feet behind him as he checked the perimeter of the tavern inside and out.

A tall man with thinning gray hair, he didn't seem to mind having a shadow. He painstakingly rattled windows, inspected sashes, jiggled locks and shone his silver flashlight into corners, behind doors and inside both restrooms.

After examining the doors and dead bolts and finding that nothing seemed to have been disturbed, he returned to the pool table where the narrow sleeping bag now lay. "You've never seen this before today?" he asked.

Lacey shook her head.

"Are you sure you didn't give out any keys to anybody? An old boyfriend, maybe?"

He was only doing his job, so she answered

his question. "I had new dead bolts installed after my father passed away. Nobody has a key except me. I know I locked the doors yesterday because I had to unlock them this afternoon before I could get in."

He turned the narrow sleeping bag upside down and gave it a little shake. A plastic bottle of water rolled out, across the floor. With a great creaking of his hips and knees, he squatted down to reach it. Hauling himself back to his feet, he unscrewed the top.

"Do you wear pink lipstick?" he asked, holding the bottle toward the light.

She shook her head and took a closer look, too. The clear plastic bottle was half-full. She recognized the brand of sparkling spring water as one sold locally, but the pale pink shade of the lip print around the top didn't look familiar to her at all.

"Frankly," Officer Pratt said, "I'm stumped. Nothing inside the tavern has been taken, broken, meddled with, defaced or damaged in any way. Judging from the size of the sleeping bag and the pink print on the bottle, it's safe to assume we're dealing with a female. I don't know how she got in and out, or why. The windows are all intact and the locks appear secure. It looks to me as if we have a Houdini on our hands. I'd call it breaking and entering, except nothing's been broken. Other than the sleeping bag and water bottle, there's not even any evidence that an actual trespassing has occurred. It feels more like a mystery than a crime, doesn't it?"

He capped his pen and closed his book, obviously finished here. She followed him to the door, where she said, "Then you're not going to do anything?"

"There's nothing more I can do," he said. "I'll make a note of your call and the subsequent findings for my report, and I'll have a patrol car drive by periodically if it'll make you feel better. Call the department if you notice anything else or if she comes back, but I don't think she will."

She thanked the policeman for coming. After he was gone, she put the cap back on the bottle and started to gather the sleeping bag into a heap for the trash. Something made her stop short of the trash can.

She hadn't heard any news reports about recent serial killers wearing pink lip gloss and sleeping under pool tables. Officer Pratt said it himself. The entire situation felt more like a mystery than a crime.

Crimes were frightening, but mysteries were, well, mysterious. The goose bumps that had been popping up all over her body dissolved. Rather than throw the items away, she shook out the bedroll and refolded it, then put it back where she'd found it under the pool table, the bottle of water with its cap screwed on tight beside it.

After cataloging everything in her mind, she turned out the lights and locked the tavern's back door. As she climbed the stairs to her apartment, she wondered if Officer Pratt was right, and whoever had visited the tavern was long gone, never to return.

Upstairs, she wandered through the little kitchen and the living room with its ancient sofa and her father's old chair. She wasn't surprised when she found herself in the tiny storage room her dad had converted into a darkroom for her when she was fourteen.

She hadn't used anything here since she'd left town two-and-a-half years ago. The amber safe light still worked and the four flat trays were stacked neatly on the counter. The enlarger, developer, chemical thermometer and the rubber-ended tongs were on the shelf where she'd left them. Maybe later she would develop the pictures she'd taken today.

The coming night no longer seemed bleak. Miraculously, neither did the immediate future.

She had a roof over her head, enough money to live on for a little while, although she was going to have to find a job soon. She had a dear, quirky friend to talk to, a mystery to ponder and a heartfelt apology from Noah to savor. Maybe there *was* a reason she was in Orchard Hill and Noah was in Orchard Hill. In her mind she pictured him as he'd looked this afternoon, a sleeping baby in one hand, his hair a little too long and his eyes hinting of intimacies they'd shared.

"People don't change," he'd said.

Perhaps not, she thought as she took the spaghetti from the refrigerator and sampled her first bite, but sometimes circumstances did. Noah had told her he was glad she was back. It was beginning to feel good to be back. And that was the last thing she'd expected.

Chapter Four

A phone was ringing. And ringing.

Lacey was leaving the restaurant on Division Street when it dawned on her that the ringing was coming from her purse. This was her first incoming call, and since only one person had her number, she said hello to April as soon as she answered.

"Any luck with your job hunt?" April asked.

"Not yet." She stepped out of the way of two customers heading for the busy restaurant. "Everyone I've talked to so far is cutting back. Rosy promised she'd call me if one of her waitresses quits. Oh, and Henry Brewbaker proposed while I was there."

Henry Brewbaker walked with a cane and tottered to The Hill for a late breakfast every morning where he had a standing order of two eggs over easy, crisp bacon and blackened toast. Not even Henry could remember exactly how old he was.

"I hate to break this to you, but Henry Brewbaker proposes to somebody at least once a day." April's laugh was cut short by a soft moan.

"Is something wrong?" Lacey asked.

"I called to tell you that your paperwork will be ready for your signature later this afternoon. Remind me to have my head examined if I ever so much as think about trying to drink you under the table again."

Lacey smiled into the phone. After she'd eaten her fill of leftover spaghetti last night, she'd walked over to April's house on Baldwin Street. April's three-year-old twins had fallen asleep in the middle of the bedtime story Lacey had been reading to them. Once the little ones had been tucked in, April had uncorked a bottle of strawberry wine and she and Lacey had talked about everything under the sun. By the second glass, April was giggling.

"No offense," Lacey said as she smoothed a crease from her navy slacks, "but you couldn't drink a teetotaler under the table."

"I know. It comes from being a preacher's daughter. You really haven't had any luck at your job hunt this morning?"

"Other than one maybe and that marriage proposal, no." Lacey had left her apartment two hours ago. So far she'd spoken with every shop owner and office manager in every business on the first five blocks of Division Street. Most were friendly and talkative, but nobody was hiring. She still had two lawyers' offices, a title company, two dress stores and a CPA firm to try.

"I'm surprised you haven't found something," April said.

"Why?"

"Because I had a dream about you last night."

Lacey was intrigued because April's dreams ranged from prophetic to unsettling to just plain weird. "You dreamed about me? What was I doing?"

"For a long time you were in the distance, lost in your reveries, walking, walking, walking. When you finally got closer, Johnny Appleseed stepped in front of you, blocking your path."

"Johnny Appleseed?" Lacey asked.

"You know, the sculpture on the town square. He came to life and handed you a sign. On one side it said Welcome Home. On the other side it said Now Hiring. That's why I was sure you'd find a job today. What else could it mean?"

"I think it means no more strawberry wine for you," Lacey said, smiling. She didn't get any arguments from April. After promising to stop by the real-estate office later to go over the listing contract, Lacey stood for a moment in front of the first dress shop she came to. She didn't know why she didn't go inside.

She started walking, walking, walking. A car backfired and easy-listening music played over the speaker on the corner. Lost in her reveries, she barely heard the sounds around her, her eyes on the bronze sculpture at the head of the town square.

Orchard Hill historians couldn't agree how long the sculpture had been standing in its place of prominence in front of the courthouse. To the residents of Orchard Hill, he was iconic. Children tried to climb him, every year the varsity football team was photographed in front of him and couples became engaged beneath him. He was often cited in directions. "When you come to the sculpture, turn right." Or "If you can see Johnny Appleseed, you've gone too far."

A whimsical fellow, the statue stood eight feet tall in patched dungarees and a tattered shirt. On his head he wore a kettle for a hat. Lacey didn't see any Welcome Home or Now Hiring signs in his outstretched hand this morning. However, she did see Noah and his brothers standing nearby.

She knew better than to stare, for staring at any of the Sullivan men was like staring at the sun. It caused her eyes to water and her head to spin far more than strawberry wine. Even after she managed to close her eyes against the onslaught of all that testosterone-laden brawn, the imprint was burned on her retinas, scratched into her brain. Nothing could have prevented her from looking again, though. This time, her gaze rested on Noah alone.

She found herself crossing the street as if she was gliding on a current of air. She didn't stop until she was three feet away.

This was a bad idea.

Noah had known it since the moment Marsh and Reed had mentioned it after they'd returned from their meeting with the P.I. in Grand Rapids yesterday. He wasn't surprised they were impressed by Sam Lafferty's probing questions, straightforward approach and expertise. It was the P.I.'s advice that they contact someone in the court system that Noah questioned. According to Sam, the youth protection agency, a branch of State Services, had the authority to swoop in and move Joey to foster care unless Marsh and Reed went through the proper channels.

"Believe me," Sam had said, "you don't want that to happen."

Reed had called their great-uncle, Judge Ivan Sullivan, and Marsh was backing the decision. Joey wasn't happy about it, and frankly, Noah didn't blame him.

The baby had started crying as soon as they'd parked in the lot fifteen minutes ago. The meeting with the judge was scheduled to begin in five minutes, and the elder Sullivan didn't take kindly to being kept waiting, great-nephews notwithstanding. They had five minutes to quiet Joey. Unfortunately, he showed no signs of relenting. His little face was red and his mouth quivered with every waaa-waaa-waaa. They'd tried feeding him, walking him, jiggling him and singing to him. He wanted nothing to do with being appeased. Noah hated to imagine what the judge was going to say about their ability to care for an infant if they couldn't find a way to comfort him by the time the meeting began.

This was a bad idea. Presenting a crying baby to the judge had as much potential for disaster as the proverbial apple cart careening downhill.

"Is something wrong with Joey?"

Noah turned at the sound of Lacey's voice. For the span of one heartbeat, everything else disappeared. There was no noise, no confusion. There was only Lacey. He was either having an embolism or a revelation.

"He won't stop crying." Reed had to raise his voice in order to be heard over the baby, who was screaming in his ear.

Noah blinked as if returning from a great

distance. When he first met Lacey, she'd worn her dark hair short. It was long and slightly wavy today. The breeze fluttered the delicate collar of her blouse, the fabric nearly the same shade of blue as her eyes.

"What have you tried?" she asked.

"Everything." This time Marsh answered. "Do you know anything about babies?"

"I know a little."

"Do you have any suggestions?" Reed asked.

Lacey held out her hands to Joey and carefully lifted him from Reed. Cradling him in her arms, she swayed to and fro and crooned unintelligible words to him, gently holding his flailing hands to his sides.

Before everyone's eyes, Joey stilled. He took one ragged breath, then another. His lips trembled, and tears matted his eyelashes, but he stopped crying. He looked up at Lacey so forlornly that Noah didn't know what to say. Marsh and Reed were in awe, too.

All around them, normal life resumed. The

bell in the nearby church tower chimed hosanna as it did every day at half-past eleven. The sun peeked through holes in the clouds like grace in old Sunday-school posters. The breeze carried the scent of the Thursday lunch special from the restaurant a block away. A panel truck rattled through the intersection. Two lawyers conversed on their way from the courthouse. Flowers bloomed along the sidewalk, and tinny music played over speakers nearby.

In the midst of it all, Noah felt the stirring of something he couldn't name. It was part desire—there was always desire when it came to Lacey—but there was something else, too, something akin to enchantment. She'd always been a looker, with her full, pouty lips and centerfold body. There was more to her than beauty, though. Sassy and witty, she could spar with the best of them. She wore sandals with cork heels and slim navy slacks that made her legs look a mile long. He'd felt those legs wrap around him many a night. There wasn't much he wouldn't give to experience that again.

"He's falling asleep," Marsh declared quietly.

"How did you do that?" Reed asked at the same time.

Noah watched Lacey as she looked down at the baby in her arms and then at Marsh, Reed and finally at him. She'd undoubtedly noticed that he hadn't spoken a word. He ran his hand along his clean-shaven jaw, and saw her taking everything in, from Marsh's black polo shirt, to Reed's tie, to Noah's white broadcloth shirt, the cuffs rolled up to his forearms.

"I learned that tactic from April," she said quietly. "Babies this small like to be wrapped up tightly. It's called swaddling. I don't have a blanket so I'm using my arms to simulate that feeling of security. Why are you three dressed up?"

"Joey has an appointment to see the judge in a few minutes."

"What did he do?" she asked.

Noah laughed out loud. The only one who reacted to her dry wit, he found himself looking into her eyes the way he gazed at the horizon, as if he could see all the way to infinity. He felt the stirring of something otherworldly again, and he didn't want it to stop.

Beside him, Marsh, who obviously had no sense of humor whatsoever today, said, "We called the judge because we have to go through the proper channels or risk the child-protection agency getting involved and taking control of Joey's care."

"We're going to be late," Reed said. "Here, Lacey. I'll take the baby."

"Wait," Noah said.

Marsh and Reed looked at him, and so did Lacey.

"You're dressed up, too," Noah said. "Do you have someplace you have to be?" The moment Lacey shook her head, he asked, "Would you do us a huge favor?"

"That's a great idea, Noah," Marsh exclaimed.

She turned her round blue eyes to each of them in silent question.

"Joey's sleeping now," Reed said quietly. "If you could hold him in the outer office while we meet with the judge in his private chambers, it would be an enormous help."

"You want me to go up to the judge's private chamber with you?" she asked.

Three tall, broad-shouldered grown men nodded in earnest. "He's squeezing our appointment in between cases," Noah explained.

It didn't take her long to make up her mind. In a matter of seconds, the entire entourage was hurrying along the curved walkway, up the courthouse steps, through the metal detectors and into the waiting elevator.

They emerged onto the third floor and arrived at the judge's office at twenty-five minutes before twelve on the nose. They were right on time.

Reed left the bag that held a spare bottle and

diaper with Lacey in the outer waiting area. Marsh knocked on the raised panel door.

While they waited for the gruff summons, Noah quietly said, "Don't stare him down. Don't fidget. And whatever you do, don't act like teenagers caught with toilet paper on a Friday night."

Reed smoothed his tie. Marsh took a deep breath.

From the other side of the door, the judge said, "Don't just stand there. Come in."

Marsh went first, and then Reed followed. After casting a look at Lacey over his shoulder, Noah went in last, closing the door behind him. In the adjoining room they fell into rank, feet apart, shoulders back, arms at their sides.

Ivan Sullivan was one of those men few people liked but nearly everyone respected. He'd earned the nickname Ivan the Terrible his first year on the bench. During his forty-year career, he'd also earned the reputation as one of the toughest, shrewdest and fairest judges in

Acorn County. Everyone, including his great-nephews, called him Judge.

In his late seventies now, his fingers were gnarled from gripping a gavel. Although his brown eyes had faded to amber, his stare was no less haughty as he gestured impatiently for each of them to sit down in one of the chairs arranged in front of his desk.

The moment they were all seated, he leveled his gaze at Noah. "I thought I told you I didn't want to see you here again."

"Yes, sir."

"How long has it been?"

"Ten years." As if the old codger didn't know exactly how long it had been since Noah had stood in his courtroom, hoping his fear didn't show.

Older now, Noah admitted that he'd been on a road to self-destruction back then. The last infraction had been for fighting. Technically, he'd been defending some young woman's honor by hitting a jerk who thought he had certain rights when it came to women who'd had a little too much to drink.

Noah hadn't known the girl, but he'd seen her struggling in the alley behind Bell's Tavern, and, hell, what choice did he have? A fight had broken out and some do-gooder called the police. It turned out the jerk had been the woman's boyfriend, and she'd refused to press charges. When the judge had pointed his gavel at Noah and asked him if he had any plans to break any more noses, he couldn't lie. He assumed he'd get slapped with a fine and maybe be sentenced to a weekend in the county jail.

Judge Sullivan had something else in mind. He gave Noah a choice: a year behind bars or a year pursuing a higher education. Noah had been stunned. The very thought of being locked up, unable to see the sky for a week, let alone for a year, had rendered him speechless, his Adam's apple wobbling and his hands shaking. At the time, the thought of being confined to a classroom had seemed nearly as confining and limiting as jail. And the judge knew it. On rare occasions, the old man had given other misunderstood and misguided hellions options that had the potential to change their lives for the better. Noah had chosen a higher education, in this case, an Airfield Operations Specialist training program open to new enrollment down in Florida. What he'd wanted to do was wipe the condescending smirk off the judge's lined face.

Ten years later, that smirk hadn't changed. Noah was smarter now and knew better than to try to stare the other man down.

Marsh began, explaining why they'd requested this meeting. Reed drew the handwritten note from Joey's mother from his pocket and slid it across the large wooden desk. Just as they'd rehearsed, they stuck to the facts about their surprising discovery of the baby on their doorstep. They described the woman Noah had seen crossing the lawn when he'd flown over, and they outlined the steps they were taking to locate Joey's mother.

The judge read the letter and turned it over much the way each of them had. "Who is she?"

This was the part that was most difficult to explain. "We're not certain," Reed said.

"What do you mean you're not certain?"

"She's either a woman from my past," Reed said quietly.

"Or a woman from mine," Marsh added.

The judge's eyes narrowed. "You're telling me you don't know which one of you is the father?"

Marsh and Reed both remained silent, the equivalent of taking the Fifth. Their discomfiture wasn't easy to witness.

"Where is the baby now?" the judge asked.

"He's in your outer office."

Noah didn't like the way the judge's lips formed a thin line. He'd seen that expression before. It meant his mind was already made up. Marsh, Reed and Noah flicked a glance at one another. Noah wasn't the only one growing more uncomfortable by the second.

"Don't just sit there," the judge said. "I want to see him."

With little choice, Marsh went to the door and opened it. "Lacey, would you bring Joey in?"

Noah and Reed rose as Lacey entered the small room. As far as Noah knew, she'd never faced a judge. Not one to let that stop her, she raised that fighter's chin of hers and strode into his chamber as if she'd done this a thousand times.

She kept her arms firmly around Joey and planted her feet well away from the judge's desk. If he wanted a closer look, he was either going to have to bid her to come closer or go to her. Noah's chest expanded again, this time with burgeoning admiration.

Judge Sullivan pushed his large leather chair back and stood, his cold, assessing, rheumy eyes on the baby in Lacey's arms. The clock ticked on the shelf beside musty old law tomes and the judge's framed law degree. For what felt like forever nobody moved.

The judge broke the silence when he said, "Take him down to State Services. I'll let them know you're coming."

Marsh backed up until he stood directly between Lacey and the judge. "All due respect, sir, no one's taking my son."

"Or mine," Reed said, going to stand beside Marsh.

"Or my nephew," Noah said, completing the wall of shoulders and determination. They remained that way, three abreast, a united front of protection for the baby they had every intention of caring for themselves.

The judge's expression didn't change, but everyone in the room felt his agitation and determination. Noah waited for the explosion.

"A baby this young needs his mother," the old man said indignantly. "At the very least, he needs to be in a woman's care, and by God—"

Before Marsh could remind their great-uncle

that he didn't have children and, therefore, was hardly an expert, and before Reed could call the judge a chauvinist and Noah could call him a lot worse, Lacey spoke up behind them. "Excuse me, Your Honor, but I am a woman."

The judge gestured impatiently with his hands. Noah took a step to the right, making room for Lacey to fall into formation between him and Marsh, Joey still fast asleep in her arms.

After looking her up and down, the judge said, "You're Harlan Bell's daughter, aren't you?"

"I'm Lacey Bell, yes." After a barely perceptible hesitation, she added, "I'm little Joseph's nanny."

The judge looked as surprised as Marsh and Reed. Noah felt a grin coming on.

"Is this true?" the judge demanded.

Since Reed and Marsh were honest to a fault, and therefore couldn't be trusted not to mess this up, Noah said, "You said it yourself, Your Honor. Babies this young need to be in a woman's care."

"Lacey is extremely good with him," Reed said, recovering.

"Have you ever heard of swaddling?" Marsh asked their uncle. "Until Lacey demonstrated and explained the technique, I never had, either. We should be getting Joey home. He'll want to eat again soon."

"Not so fast."

Noah, Marsh and Reed didn't move. Lacey broke away from the others and came to stand directly in front of the judge's desk. "Would you like to hold your great-great-nephew, Your Honor?"

The judge took his wire-rimmed glasses off, cleaned them and put them back on. Even Noah was having a hard time refraining from fidgeting.

After what felt like a very long time, Judge Sullivan said, "No, I would not. He does look like a Sullivan, I'll give him that."

For a moment, Noah almost thought the judge was going to say something complimentary or perhaps bestow some memory of their child-hoods, or his. Instead, he said, "I expect a weekly progress report and a phone call the moment you locate his mother."

"Yes, sir." Marsh opened the door.

"Thank you, sir," Reed said, gesturing for Lacey to precede him from the room.

Lacey carried the baby out, Reed right behind her, followed by Marsh. The last one through the door, Noah couldn't be sure whether the judge was hiding a smug smile or indigestion.

Noah wasn't prone to smiles, either, but he couldn't keep a grin off his face as he followed the others back the way they'd come, through the judge's outer office, down the long corridor, into the elevator, out through the lobby, down the courthouse steps and out into the valiant un-folding of a mild but far-from-ordinary summer day.

He'd never put a lot of faith in Fate. In his experience, life randomly knocked people on their ass. Those who could hauled themselves back to their feet and those who couldn't either crawled to a safe corner or gave up.

Lacey was a fighter. They were alike that way. He'd said it yesterday. It was good to have her back in town. Orchard Hill hadn't been the same without her. And neither had he.

As he followed Lacey and his brothers to the bronze Johnny Appleseed sculpture, he realized that he wanted another chance with her. He wasn't sure how to go about it. They couldn't just pick up where they'd left off. Their differences were still between them. Where exactly did that leave them?

Lacey could feel three sets of eyes on her back. She was accustomed to that. She turned around and faced Noah and his brothers. "This is where I came in," she said. "Who wants to take the baby?"

Marsh and Reed both held out their hands for Joey. It occurred to her that one of them was going to be terribly disappointed before this situation was resolved.

"Why don't you give him to me?" Noah said.

The transfer was handled a little awkwardly but safely. Joey woke up, but he didn't cry. He looked around, unbelievably tiny, but perfect in every way. Her heart gave a little thump, because babies were miracles. Joey was extremely alert. It seemed to Lacey that he was already starting to recognize all three of the Sullivan men. It was almost as if he realized he was one of them, a throwback to past generations of rugged, smart Sullivans.

"I don't know how to thank you," Marsh said.

"You were amazing, Lacey," Reed added.

"I, for one, am not surprised," Noah said, his voice huskier than the others'.

She could hold her own with nearly anybody, but even she got a little breathless when these three turned on the charm at the same time. Flexing the kink out of her arm now that she was no longer holding Joey, she said, "You can have me canonized, throw quarters, whatever, but, for the record, you're welcome. I just hope I don't go to jail for lying to a judge."

"It doesn't have to be a lie," Reed said.

She tilted her head ever so much and backed up a step. "I have to find a job. That's what I was doing when you shanghaied me."

"That's what I mean," he said. "It pains me to admit it, but the judge was right. We're in over our heads. Joey needs a nanny. We need a nanny for him. We'll pay you."

She caught a movement out of the corner of her eye. Marsh and Noah flashed each other a quick glance.

"Reed," Noah said.

"Reed's right," Marsh insisted.

"Guys," Noah said, more firmly this time.

"But I haven't had any official training as a nanny," she stammered.

"He likes you," Reed stated. "That's all that matters."

"But…"

"Before you arrived this morning, none of us

could do a thing to calm him," Reed said. "He responds to you, Lacey. Maybe it's your scent or the sound of your voice or your gentle touch."

Lacey couldn't hide her surprise. Her—Joey's nanny? It was ludicrous.

If Marsh was the rule breaker and Noah the risk taker, Reed, the golden-haired son, was the smooth talker. There was an unmistakable earnestness on his face as he added, "You said it yourself. You're looking for a job. Come to work for us as Joey's nanny."

"Even if you would just agree to a temporary position," Marsh said, as earnest as Reed. "We'll make it worth your while."

Noah was noticeably silent.

After a brief discussion with Reed, Marsh named a dollar amount that widened her eyes. It was far more than she would earn waitressing or working at the clothing store or as an administrative assistant, provided somebody actually hired her.

"Define *temporary*," she said in spite of herself.

Again, Marsh and Reed spoke among themselves for a moment. Evidently, having reached a consensus, Reed said, "Whatever you can give us, we'll appreciate. A day, a week, indefinitely or just until I've had a chance to place an ad and we hire a permanent nanny."

"What hours are you thinking?" she asked.

At the same time, Marsh and Reed both smiled.

"What hours do you want?" Marsh asked.

"How soon can you start?" Reed added.

"Tomorrow morning?" she asked.

Marsh tipped his face to the sun and laughed for the first time in days. Out of the blue, he swooped down, wrapped his arms around her waist and spun her off her feet. She'd no sooner touched the ground before Reed spun her, too. Dizzy, she noticed Noah standing to one side, the baby in his arms, a pensive expression on his face.

"We'll see you tomorrow," Marsh declared. The next thing she knew, all three of the Sullivans were turning around and heading toward the parking lot west of the courthouse.

Slightly dazed, she started in the opposite direction. She happened to glance up at the bronze sculpture as she passed. At that exact moment, a single ray of sunshine poked between two clouds and slanted toward the sculpture like a staircase to heaven. Johnny Appleseed winked.

She stopped and stared. Then blinked. "An optical illusion. A trick of the sun. Just my imagination," she murmured under her breath.

As she meandered back the way she'd come, she had to pinch herself. Sculptures didn't wink and sunbeams were not staircases to heaven. She couldn't discount one coincidence, though. One minute she'd been looking for a job, and seemingly the next she'd agreed to become little Joey Sullivan's temporary nanny. Strangely, April's dream had come true.

She recalled how quiet Noah had grown when

Reed had made the suggestion. Something was on his mind. Was he thinking about the night they broke up? Was he remembering that kiss the night before last? Or was he wondering, as she was, if they dared try again? She had no idea what that would entail, or if it was even possible. And, yet, she was thinking about it.

Chicago was a bustling, vibrant city, but nobody she knew had discovered a baby on a doorstep there. Sculptures there didn't wink and mysterious escape artists didn't sleep under pool tables. She'd lived there for over two years, but during that time she'd never experienced this giddy sense of anticipation, as if anything was possible.

Chapter Five

For nearly two years, Noah had been painstakingly restoring an old Piper Cherokee in one of Tom Bender's spare hangars. A lifelong dream, it required an aptitude for aerodynamics, an innate knowledge of the mechanics of moving parts and unfailing patience. So the fact that he'd spent the past hour assembling baby furniture wasn't the reason he felt like biting through his cheek.

He'd had an errand to run after the meeting with the judge, and had gotten home twenty minutes behind the others. A delivery truck had been pulling out of the driveway as he was driving in. Now the entire first floor looked like Christmas morning in a war zone. That didn't bother him, either.

Last night Reed had ordered nearly every imaginable baby item they could possibly need from a local store. There were boxes of disposable diapers, baby clothes, toys, a wireless baby monitor, two more car seats, a baby swing, a mobile, discarded cardboard, cellophane and packing foam, and baby furniture in various stages of assembly.

On baby duty this afternoon, Reed had Joey with him in his home office off the living room at the front of the house. Marsh and Noah were on the floor in the den, a room they were converting into a daytime nursery. At night Joey would sleep upstairs in the heirloom cradle Marsh had found in the attic on the baby's first night here.

The changing table and dresser were

assembled. Noah was working on the baby swing. Next to him, Marsh was rereading the directions for the crib.

"Hand me those pliers," Noah said.

Marsh was studying the directions and didn't hear him. What else was new? It rankled, but then, Noah had been stewing ever since they'd left Lacey in the courthouse square.

"If you have something to say, say it," Marsh said without looking up.

So he *had* noticed.

"It's a little late to ask for my input now, isn't it?"

"What's your problem?" Marsh turned the directions over noisily. "Tell me you're not jealous because I hugged your girlfriend."

"Jealous of you?" Noah decided not to even address the fact that she wasn't his girlfriend. He was still eyeing the pliers that were lying on the other side of Marsh's knee. Beside him Marsh wadded the directions into a ball. He supposed he should have taken that as a hint that Marsh's patience was wearing thin. But Noah wasn't in the mood to take hints.

He admitted that he *could* have been more careful when he reached for the pliers. Maybe the way he *accidentally* bumped Marsh with his shoulder could have been construed as a *slight* shove. Marsh *probably* meant to give him only a little push in return. But Noah was on his haunches and the return jostle caused him to lose his balance. He automatically grabbed Marsh's arm. Unfortunately, Marsh was on the balls of his feet, too.

The two of them toppled backward, landing with a crash on discarded cardboard and packaging foam. Marsh went up on one elbow. Noah sat up and brushed himself off, prepared to get back to work.

"Not so fast, flyboy." Marsh threw his arm around Noah's chest and pulled him backward.

Noah's surprise lasted just long enough to glimpse the confidence on his brother's face. As the oldest, Marsh apparently assumed he had the upper hand, the way he had when they were kids. Noah wasn't smaller anymore, but he was still six years younger, an asset now if there ever was one. He was more agile, too, not to mention more experienced in fighting. He was going to enjoy pinning Marsh until he cried uncle.

Marsh had something else in mind. He drove that fact home when Noah landed with a loud thump on his back on the floor. Letting loose a war cry, Noah got serious. Marsh didn't stay on top for long. They rolled around on the floor, grunting when an elbow was jabbed into an opponent's midsection and knees collided and heads knocked. The wrestling match got rowdier and the banging and thumping and slamming of bodies into furniture louder.

"What's going on?" It seemed that Reed had come to investigate the racket.

"Noah started it."

"The hell I did."

Reed planted his Cole Haans and folded his

arms. He was the only person Noah knew who could look down his nose at somebody with his nose still in the air.

"If you're going to behave like children," he said, "take it outside."

"Where's Joey?" Marsh asked.

"He's asleep in my office."

Marsh and Noah looked at each other. At the same time, they lunged toward Reed.

He toppled like a stack of building blocks. "Are you both out of your minds? Ooof. Get off me."

"What's the matter? Afraid to get your chinos wrinkled?" Marsh asked.

"Or are you just afraid to lose?" Noah added.

Those were fighting words. The years fell away, along with Reed's air of polish and sophistication. He dived into the foray with all the gusto of a street fighter.

The exercise caused an adrenaline rush that invigorated all three of them. A one-on-one skirmish was a fair match. This was every man for himself. Whoever was on top of the heap was winning. That changed too often to track. Arms and legs got tangled, expletives exchanged and retaliation promised. If the momentum hadn't sent them careening into the end table, which in turn sent a lamp crashing to the floor, there was no telling who would have come out ahead.

The explosion of ceramic and shattering glass had the effect of a bell at a boxing match. It officially ended the round. Noah had Reed in a headlock, Reed had Marsh's left leg bent like a pretzel and Marsh had an arm around Noah's chest. It took a little doing to get untangled.

Free at last, Reed sat up. "What in the world is going on with you two?" he asked as he examined his shirt and chinos for damage.

"Noah has something to say to us," Marsh said as if the scuffle hadn't interrupted the conversation.

Reed looked sideways at Noah. "Let's hear it."

Still on his back on the floor, Noah tested

his legs to see if they would straighten out. "I just made the last payment on the loan for my Airfield Operations Specialist training."

"A fight broke out over that?" With a slight groan, Reed rolled up on all fours. "You should be celebrating."

"Lacey was the first person I wanted to tell." When Noah had found the training program open to new enrollment down in Florida ten years ago, Marsh and Reed had wanted to help him find a way to pay for the expensive course, but Noah had already owed them for giving up their futures for him, and even if he could have let them do more, Noah had needed to prove to them and to himself that he could do it his own way, to try to succeed on his own. He'd found another lender, and had been diligently paying it off for nine years.

Reed was right; it was cause for celebration. "So tell her," he said.

"I can't, thanks to the two of you. She would think it had more to do with gratitude because she agreed to be Joey's temporary nanny." Noah wanted something a hell of a lot more substantial than gratitude. "We dodged a bullet with the judge because of her."

"She saved our asses," Marsh agreed.

"And Joey," Reed said reverently.

"You should have asked me before you coerced her into accepting the position as Joey's nanny."

Marsh stared at Noah from his feet, Reed from his knees. "You're angry because we didn't consult you first?" Reed asked.

"I'd probably have a heart attack if you ever did that." He could tell he'd struck a nerve. "Expecting Lacey to be Joey's nanny was unfair to her, especially considering the reason we broke up."

Marsh stopped tucking his shirt in long enough to share a look with Reed. "Why *did* you two break up?"

Noah was sorry he'd brought it up. Until now he'd kept the reason vague, saying they'd wanted different things. Taking a deep breath, he blurted, "Because she wanted kids."

Marsh looked at Noah as if something was finally starting to make sense. "You mean you don't?" he asked kindly.

Noah didn't reply.

"Have you always felt this way?" Marsh continued in the same patient tone of voice.

"Don't psychoanalyze me, okay?"

On his feet now, too, Reed said, "Noah? Have you?"

When they were kids, it seemed that one or another of them was always getting caught someplace they shouldn't have been, doing something they shouldn't have been doing. Rather than lie when questioned by an adult, they'd developed a little gesture that entailed shrugging just one shoulder. It meant *I'd rather not say*. Noah demonstrated it now.

Marsh's sigh came from a place deep inside him. "I always worried that the chances you took with your life and your future had to do with being in the car with Mom and Dad that day."

Reed was watching Noah as intently as Marsh was. "It wasn't your fault, buddy," Reed said. "You couldn't have prevented what happened."

Their dad used to call Noah *buddy*. Hearing it again caught him below his breastbone. "I know that."

"I would have bet money on the fact that you were disappointed when you found out Joey wasn't yours," Marsh said.

"Yeah," he said, sitting up. "Nobody was more surprised about that than me."

Marsh and Reed each held out a hand and practically launched Noah to his feet. "Are you saying you've changed your mind?" Marsh asked now that they were all looking eye to eye.

"I made a vow the day we buried Mom and Dad."

"It sounds to me as if you made a *decision*," Reed countered. "A decision based on witnessing a tragedy no fifteen-year-old should ever witness."

Other than the time he'd told Lacey, Noah never talked about the day his parents died. He didn't talk about the funeral, either, or how utterly empty and silent the house and the orchard had been after their parents were suddenly just gone. Everything had changed, and that, in turn, changed the three of them and their younger sister, Madeline. That wasn't what was at the front of his mind today. "It's been two-and-a-half years since Lacey left," he said. "I don't even know how she feels about me anymore."

"How do you feel about her?" Reed asked.

"Are you in love with her?" Marsh said, more to the point.

"She's in my blood. Either of you ever have that happen?"

Marsh said nothing.

Reed shrugged one shoulder much as Noah had a moment ago. "Maybe you should ask her if she feels the same way about you," he said.

This from a man who hadn't thought to get the last name of the woman he'd slept with and possibly fathered a child with. All his life Noah had been the wiry kid brother everybody worried about, while rugged, man-of-the-earth Marsh had the patience of a saint and brainy, brawny Reed was shamelessly self-confident. Joey's unexpected arrival was leveling the playing field.

"Maybe we *should* have consulted you before asking Lacey to accept the job as Joey's nanny," Marsh said. "But she doesn't strike me as the type of woman who would do something she doesn't want to do."

Noah was reminded of the other night when she'd opened her door, tears in her eyes. He'd reached for her hand, put his arms around her and kissed her. She *had* reacted, turning warm and pliant and oh-so-willing. Passion had flamed between them straight to inferno level.

"You might want to grab some ice for that cracked lip before you pay her another visit," Reed said as if he'd read Noah's mind.

Gingerly touching his sore lip with one finger, Noah looked around the room. A sense of calm was settling over him. He recalled the silent promise he'd made the day he'd watched his parents' caskets being lowered into the ground. Joey's arrival was causing him to question his stand. It scared the spit out of him, but it wasn't enough to keep him from wanting to knock on Lacey's door all over again.

"We got lucky today," he said. "Let's get this nursery finished for Joey before the judge decides to send somebody out here for a surprise home visit."

Marsh and Reed both shuddered.

Hunkering down in front of the baby swing he'd been assembling when that little fight broke out, Noah recalled how Lacey's voice had sounded today after the judge had proclaimed that babies needed a woman's care. "Your Honor," she'd said, "I am a woman."

She was a woman, all right—an amazing one—but he couldn't just race over to her place and haul her off to bed. As tempting as that notion was, he couldn't burn this passion off as if sex was enough.

She *was* in his blood. Two-and-a-half years apart hadn't diminished that. If she was going to give him another chance she was going to need a good reason. He couldn't fly by the seat of his pants this time. Winning her back would require careful thought and a well-devised plan.

She would be here in the morning. That didn't leave him much time.

He set the baby swing upright and viewed his handiwork. Marsh fished the wadded-up directions from the other debris. Reed returned with a broom and dustpan and started cleaning up the broken lamp. Noah noticed that Reed was favoring his right elbow and Marsh was limping. Had it not been for his cracked lip, Noah would have smiled.

They would all be sore tomorrow. They weren't kids anymore. Despite an occasional sojourn back to adolescence, like the one they'd taken a few minutes ago, they were grown-ups. He didn't know when that had happened. Even more astonishing, when had he started thinking like one?

Lacey waved goodbye to Miss Fergusson, the administrator of the Orchard Hill Public Library, and with her stack of library books tucked under one arm, started toward home.

The evening was balmy and the sun still bright in the western sky. Lacey loved this time of year in Michigan when it stayed light until nearly ten o'clock. It was eight now. The library was closing. Many of the other businesses were rolling up their sidewalks, too. In a little while, April and her sister-in-law were stopping over with the for-sale signs for the tavern's windows.

Since she'd been back, Lacey had noticed that the women in Jay's family fussed over April like mother hens. After her mom's death, Lacey had received her mothering from more unexpected sources. She'd been introduced to the

"It takes a village to raise a child" philosophy shortly after she and her dad moved to Orchard Hill when she was twelve. Miss Fergusson had noticed her sneaking a book off a library shelf and followed her to the bathroom. Blushing to the roots of her steel-gray hair, the stern, no-nonsense librarian had assured Lacey that she wasn't dying. The bleeding was *normal.*

Lacey had been unabashedly relieved, until Miss Fergusson explained about Mother Nature's monthly gift. "Every month?" Lacey had quipped. "Are you frickin' kidding me?"

"You're becoming a woman," Miss Fergusson had declared with a smile that had grown brighter before Lacey's eyes. "And that's a marvelous, beautiful creature, indeed."

Six months ago, two emergency surgeries days apart had left Lacey feeling the opposite of beautiful. The angry red scars on her belly were slowly fading, just as her doctor had promised. Although there had been internal scarring, too, and she couldn't forget the impact the scarring had on her future, every day she felt a little more like her old self.

The evening stretched languidly before her. She still hadn't developed those photographs of Joey, and now she had books to read, too. Trying to decide whether she should begin with the *Hands-On Guide to Infant Child Care* or delve into the two hardcovers about Houdini and modern-day escape artists, she darted across First Street. She hadn't gone far when she heard a horn honk behind her.

She glanced over her shoulder as a dusty-blue pickup truck pulled to a stop at the curb beside her. She knew that Chevy well.

The grin Noah slanted her made him appear relaxed and sinuous, like an alley cat taking a break from his tomcatting to stretch languidly in a warm patch of sunshine. "Need a lift?" he called through the open passenger window.

"Thanks, but I'm only two blocks from home."

He continued to stare at her. In the ensuing silence, she backed up a few steps. When he still made no move to leave, she said, "Is something wrong?"

"Not really."

Homing in on his mouth, she said, "What happened to your lip?"

"I ran into something." He tilted his head self-mockingly. "I've narrowed it down to either Marsh's elbow or Reed's knee."

Obviously, it had been a guy thing, but she had to ask, "Did you win?"

"It was a three-way tie."

"What were you fighting about?" she asked.

"We were just burning off steam. You know how guys are, although, if you must know, they aren't making it easy for me to gallop in on my great white steed and rescue you from a future of celibacy and regret."

She glanced over her shoulder as a group of teenage boys too young to drive ambled by on their way to wherever teenage boys went on balmy Thursday nights these days. Rather than continue this conversation where anyone could hear, she strolled to Noah's open passenger-side window. "Excuse me, did you say celibacy and regret?"

He gave her a crooked smile that went straight to her head. "Today I made the final payment on the loan for my Airfield Operations Specialist training," he said.

She knew Noah well enough to understand that he was a man of few words. And while that didn't always make his conversation easy to follow, what he said eventually fit together like pieces of a beautiful puzzle.

"You're free, Noah. It's what you've always wanted."

"I'd like to talk to you about that."

His gaze was as soft as a caress and almost as possessive. He wanted her. Being wanted by him sent those butterflies fluttering their naughty little wings again.

"Digger found a used propeller for the old airplane we're restoring," he said, his voice deepening as if he felt those butterflies, too. "He picked it up over in Rockford today. I was on my way to the airstrip to take a look at it. Care to ride along?"

"I ca—"

"If you'd rather just grab a beer, or something to eat, I'll call Dig and reschedule."

She was shaking her head before he'd completed the invitation. She thought about those scars and hospital bills. Noah might be free, but she wasn't. "I can't just forget everything that's happened, Noah."

"That's just it," he said. "I can't forget, either. Any of it. Not how good we were together, not how much I've missed you, not how damn good it is to see you do something as ordinary as walk down the sidewalk. Come on, Lace. Come for a drive with me."

His eyes reminded her of the heat lightning that flickered on the horizon on sweltering summer nights. More often than not that lightning continued dancing in the distance, hinting at relief without making any promises of rain. From now on she needed promises.

Pushing away slightly from his dusty pickup truck, she said, "April and her sister-in-law are coming over. They're probably waiting for me now. I really do have to go."

She didn't know why her heart was racing as she turned on her heel, but the need to flee was instinctive and strong. She waited until she'd reached the end of the block to look behind her. The dusty-blue Chevy was no longer idling at the curb. Noah was gone.

With a deep, calming breath, she resumed her trek toward the apartment she once again called home. She took a shortcut through the hardware store the way she used to. As she wended her way through a maze of aisles, she faced the fact that she wasn't fleeing from Noah. She was running from her feelings for him. It would be so much easier if he didn't bring out every yearning for happily-ever-after she'd ever had.

She walked around a display of box fans and past bins containing nuts and bolts, electrical wire and plumbing supplies, and emerged into the alley, two stores away from her own back door. She hadn't taken more than half a dozen steps when she stopped in her tracks.

That dusty-blue Chevy was sitting in her dad's old parking space. Noah leaned against the tailgate, his arms folded and his ankles crossed, giving the illusion that he'd been waiting for a long time.

Although the sun was still shining on the other side of the brick buildings lining Division Street, dusk had fallen here in the alley. Shadows stretched from end to end, deeper and darker in the narrow spaces between buildings, in doorways and beneath stairs.

"Where's your dad's truck?" Noah asked, letting his arms fall to his sides.

"I sold it two days ago." Her voice sounded normal. At least something functioned normally. "Noah, what are you doing here?"

* * *

Noah admitted that it was a legitimate question. The truth was, he hadn't planned to come here tonight. When he'd left the orchard after dinner, he'd assumed he had another twelve hours before he began laying the foundation for a future with Lacey. Then he'd seen her when he'd turned onto First Street. And now here he was, twelve hours ahead of schedule.

She'd exchanged her navy slacks for gray shorts that hugged her hips and showcased a pair of legs that should have been outlawed. He'd never met another woman who caused his hormones this much commotion just by walking down the sidewalk. He could see the butterfly tattoo on her right foot from here. It matched the yellow nail polish on her toes. Another tiny butterfly was hidden beneath the waistband of her shorts. He remembered it well.

Before every last drop of the blood rushing through his ears ended up south of there, he strolled closer. Lacey held her ground. Damn, she was something.

"We can't just pick up where we left off, Noah. Real life isn't like a fairy tale." She held up one hand. "Stop right there."

He didn't stop until the tips of his shoes touched the tips of hers, their bodies so close he felt her heat and she felt his. She wanted to know what he was doing here. That much he knew. He was going to kiss her. And, if he was lucky, she was going to let him.

He didn't say anything as he placed a hand on either side of her face, his fingers splaying wide in her hair, his thumbs resting lightly along the outer edges of her cheekbones. Her eyes looked violet in this light, blurring before his as he tipped her head up slightly. Slowly, he covered her mouth with his. He heard her breath catch. And then her eyes fluttered closed.

Her lips were warm and soft and wet, and tasted like cinnamon candy, her favorite. Sampled this way, it was his favorite, too. He moved his mouth over her sweet lips, again and again and again, a gentle persuasion that somehow translated into an unspoken how do you do.

It was just supposed to be a kiss, and yet it made sense out of nothing, gave rhyme to reason and changed the beating rhythm of his heart. Heat coursed through him, converging at the very center of him, tempting him to wrap his arms around her and fit her soft curves where need was demanding attention. My, was he tempted.

For what seemed like an eternity, she remained motionless, her face tipped up, her mouth open slightly beneath his, breathlessly accepting his kiss. Then he felt it, the tentative touch of her fingertips as she placed her hands over his. He offered up a silent prayer of thanksgiving for granting him this moment.

He'd kissed Lacey a thousand times, but he'd never kissed her quite like this. It might have gone down in history for its richness, its purity and its sweetness. All the while, their only points of contact were their lips, his hands on her face and her hands on his.

Muffled laughter and what sounded a little like a stampede of elephants ended the kiss. When Lacey opened her eyes, she saw those teenage boys again. They were running through the alley, trying their darnedest to keep from snickering.

They weren't the only ones taking this short-cut. A slender young woman stepped aside, quietly letting the guys pass. There was something about her that held Lacey spellbound. It was hard to tell how old she was in this light. She wore jeans and a black T-shirt. The bill of a dark baseball cap was pulled low over her forehead. Unlike the boys, she kept her head down as she hurried by.

Realizing that she and Noah were still standing toe-to-toe, her face still in his big hands, her hands still on his, Lacey finally came to her senses. She took a step back. Her arms fell to her sides and so did his. They dragged in deep breaths, as if they'd forgotten to breathe until now.

"Well," she said.

His grin reminded them both of his sore lip.

"Does it hurt?" she asked.

"What, my lip?"

Okay, the Noah she knew was back. She tilted her head abruptly and slanted him a look that spoke volumes.

Noah shrugged those amazing shoulders of his. Running his hand over his jaw, he said, "Honestly? I forgot about my lip until now. That was great therapy. I'd like to try it again."

The need to flee had returned. This time she stood her ground and said, "But we're two different people now."

"You're still you and I'm still me. It's safe to say a passion like ours hasn't evaporated into thin air."

"Now you're playing it *safe?*" she asked.

"Leave it to you to choose *that* word out of all the others to call me on."

At least sparring with him was in her comfort zone. Sharing sweet kisses that made her feel beautiful and wish she believed in fairy tales like the ones she'd read to April's twins last night wasn't.

Tomorrow she was going to the Sullivan household where she would assume the role of Joey's temporary nanny. Before that occurred, there was something she needed to say, a point she had to make. "We can't pick up where we left off, Noah. We can't go back. Nobody can."

Widening his stance slightly, he rested his hands lightly on his hips and met her gaze. "I was going to wait until tomorrow to talk to you about this, but you might as well know I have no intention of going back to the beginning."

"At least we agree on some—"

"And you're right. We can't just pick up where we left off over two years ago, or last year, either."

She drew her eyebrows down, a no-no according to the beauty magazines. She forgot why. "Then what was that kiss?"

"That's what I wanted to talk to you about," he said, his grin slow and sincere. "Years from now we'll look back on this day. Because today is the day we began anew."

He gave her that smile again, the one that reminded her of an alley cat stretching languidly in a glorious patch of sunshine. Darned if her insides didn't stretch a little, too.

"That kiss," he said, his gaze settling on her mouth, "was the beginning of our new beginning."

There was something about the way he'd spoken that sounded like the prequel to happily-ever-after. She really needed different reading material. Nobody lived happily ever after. If people were lucky, they lived happily-sometimes-after. That brought her back to the beginning.

While she was still standing there, her heart speeding up and slowing down by turns, an

Oldsmobile with an engine knock pulled up alongside Noah's Chevy. April threw the gearshift into Park and cut the engine.

Each of the Avery brood had learned to drive in that car. Although the mishaps and the wear and tear showed, it still had a few good years and a lot of miles left in it. With the youngest off to London for the summer, April's mother-in-law had assured Lacey that she was more than happy to let her borrow it. That was the kind of good people there were in Orchard Hill, in Michigan, in the world. They were "It takes a village" people—kind, thoughtful ordinary people who made others feel just a little extraordinary.

April was opening the door of the car she was dropping off for Lacey to drive, as her sister-in law pulled up in a shiny new SUV. "Sorry to interrupt," she said, smiling at Lacey and Noah.

Had everyone seen that kiss?

April's sister-in-law got out, too. With a knowing little smile that was an answer to

Lacey's silent question, Gabby Avery pushed her chin-length blond hair behind her ears and opened the back of her SUV. Suddenly, Noah was there, hauling out the for-sale signs they were going to place in the tavern's front and back windows.

The man had a rangy physique—there was no doubt about it. His jeans were faded at the major stress points: knees, pockets and fly. His split lip lent the ultimate authenticity to his bad-boy persona.

"You didn't interrupt, April," he said as he carried the signs past her and leaned them against the tavern's back door. "I was leaving. Tell Jay hi for me, okay?"

"I will, Noah, thanks."

His gaze rested on Lacey for a heartbeat longer than the others. "Do you need a ride in the morning?"

Lacey shook her head and managed to say, "I've got it covered."

"Then I'll see you tomorrow."

With a swagger that made all three of them salivate, he sauntered to his pickup and got in. In no time at all he'd started the engine and backed out of his parking spot.

Gabby Avery was ten years older than Lacey and April, and had been happily married to Jay's oldest brother for eight years. Obviously, that hadn't prevented her from appreciating the view. She fanned herself with one hand and said, "What on earth was that?"

For a moment Lacey paused, on the brink of the precipice that was the rest of her life. Before her was the unknown with all its wonder and risk. She could turn her back on all of it. Or she could take the next step into the unknown. The choice was hers.

In her mind she saw herself testing for solid footing with the tips of her toes. "If I'm not mistaken," Lacey said, watching until Noah's taillights disappeared around the corner, "that was the beginning of the new beginning of Noah and me."

* * *

"Ow."

"What happened?" April asked.

"It was just my finger," her sister-in-law said. "Don't worry. I don't use that one much anyway."

The two of them were at the front window in Bell's Tavern, trying their darnedest to fasten the for-sale sign with its fancy Avery Realty logo and phone number to the window frame. The board wasn't heavy; it was cumbersome, bulky and a tad unruly. Lacey had tried to help. When it became apparent that she was only getting in the way, she'd left the installation to the experts.

"Ow." This time it was April who pinched her poor finger.

Smiling to herself, Lacey thought that perhaps *experts* wasn't the proper term. The lights were on in the tavern and the back door was propped open. After casually checking the window locks and finding them all intact, Lacey wandered to the pool table in the back of the room.

She hadn't been down here since Officer Pratt had taken a look around. It wasn't that she hadn't thought about it. She just hadn't quite gotten up the nerve to venture down here alone. She wondered if Officer Pratt had been right, and whoever had been here was long gone by now.

Far away from the thumps and thuds at the front window, she peeked under the pool table. The sleeping bag was still there, pretty much where it had been the other night. It was difficult to tell if it had been slept in, but the water bottle was gone. A partially empty bag of cashews and a half-full bottle of green tea were now beside the sleeping bag.

Biting her lip to stifle the little buzz of excitement running through her, she cast another look to the front window to make sure April and Gabby weren't looking. Confident that the coast was clear, she swooped down for a closer look at the little nest that had been created here.

A strand of hair on the edge of the bedroll caught her eye. Grasping it between her thumb and forefinger, she brought it closer for a better look. Lacey's hair skimmed her shoulders. This strand was twice that long.

Her Houdini had been back. Once again she'd come and gone without breaking a window or leaving any clue as to how she was getting in and out.

Little by little, Lacey felt as if she was becoming acquainted with her guest. Although she was still no closer to discovering her Houdini's actual identity, Lacey knew she wore pink lip gloss and had long brown hair. She didn't leave a mess, and apparently she liked healthy snacks.

She must be very brave to live as she was living. Lacey was beginning to think that perhaps she wasn't the only woman in Orchard Hill poised on the brink of beginning anew.

Chapter Six

Traffic on Old Orchard Highway wasn't heavy at twenty minutes after eight on Friday morning. The window on the passenger side of the car Lacey was borrowing from April's in-laws wouldn't go all the way up, and the seat only latched in two places, but the car started on the first try, the brakes were new and the radio got fantastic reception.

It had rained during the night. Now the sun was shining, turning the moisture on the ground into vapors that shimmered like radio waves in the distance. At the River Bridge, she slipped on a pair of sunglasses, cranked up the radio and crested a hill, leaving her stomach behind.

That might have been nerves. Or anticipation.

Before she fell asleep last night, she'd taken a personality quiz in a fashion magazine. The twenty questions were an eclectic mix of random information: How many letters were in her name? What was worse—spiders or snakes? Did she dream in color? Had she ever had an encounter with an alien or settled a dispute using rock, paper and scissors? That sort of thing. According to the "scientific" results, she wasn't a morning person. She'd known that before sharpening her pencil, but a little validation never hurt anybody.

Being a night owl hadn't prevented her from jumping up at the crack of dawn this morning and preparing to begin her new job. Nothing could have prevented her from dreaming about new beginnings and Noah's kiss. She couldn't help wondering what the day would bring.

Just then, the orchard came into view. The first driveway followed the east property line and ended in a large clearing that bordered the stone cider house and the whitewashed bakery barn and the shed where homemade apple cider and doughnuts were sold to the throngs of people who swarmed here every autumn. Lacey turned into the second drive. Secluded and private, it led to the big Victorian house at the top of the hill.

Pea gravel crunched beneath her tires as she pulled up beside Noah's truck. She finger-combed her hair and straightened her clothes. With everything she would need to begin her new job stacked neatly in her arms, she went to the back door.

One thing she didn't have was a spare hand to knock. "Hello?" she called.

Hearing no answering call telling her to come in, she stood for a moment looking through the screen. The coffeemaker was gurgling noisily on the counter in the kitchen. A chair had been left out. It appeared to hold the spillover of baby clothes from the table.

"Anybody home?" she said softly, in case Joey was sleeping.

Of course they were home. The door was open and the coffee was brewing and Marsh, Reed and Noah's vehicles were all in the driveway.

"Hello?" she called again.

After a little finagling to free one hand, she let herself in. Now that she was inside, she could hear faint masculine voices. They seemed to be coming from the front of the house. Leaving the bowl she was returning on the counter and her purse, camera, library books and the little gift she'd brought stacked neatly on the table, she went in search of whoever was in charge.

"Marsh, is that you?" Reed called.

Expecting Lacey any minute, Noah had been on his way to the kitchen, but hearing Reed calling, he stuck his arms into the sleeves of his clean T-shirt and cut across the living room instead. He found Reed sitting behind his desk in his home office, Joey sucking noisily on his bottle.

"I just met Marsh on the front stairs," Noah said. "Do you need something?"

"Go get him. Tell him it's important."

Noah had taken Joey's four-o'clock feeding, but the tone of Reed's voice was quickly dissolving his grogginess. Marsh must have heard it, too, because he was suddenly in the doorway beside Noah.

"An email just came in from that P.I. Sam Lafferty," Reed said. "Take a look at this."

Marsh and Noah crowded behind Reed's desk and looked at his computer screen. The three of them practically knocked heads as they leaned closer to the monitor where there were several photographs of a dark-haired woman. While they were studying the pictures, the phone on the desk rang.

Reed answered, listened intently and promptly said, "He and Noah are both here, Sam. I'm putting you on speakerphone." He pushed a button and, when Joey started to fuss, reached for the forgotten bottle and offered it to the baby once again. Joey forgave him as soon as he had the nipple in his mouth.

"The pictures on your screen are of a woman named Julia Monroe," Sam said. "She just went into a little bungalow on a tree-lined street here in Charleston. Of the six women with that name I found in West Virginia, three are in the right age bracket. This is the only brunette. If she's not the right Julia Monroe, there are more in Florida, Alabama and Tennessee. There are likely others but I'm starting here because you said she had a soft Southern accent and that she mentioned growing up in West Virginia. Is it her, Marsh?"

Marsh studied the screen. "It might be. Her hair was long when I knew her."

Marsh took a closer look at the pictures of a woman with extremely short hair. Once again, Sam's voice sounded over the speaker. "A new hairstyle can completely change a woman's appearance. Look carefully at her face, her clothes and her build, anything that might trigger recognition."

"I can't be sure from this angle," Marsh said. "Can you get a picture from the front?"

Just then Noah noticed a movement in the doorway. Lacey paused there, taking everything in.

For Noah, time stood still.

Once, a guy he knew down in Ohio told him about a phenomenon he described as feeling thunderstruck. He said one minute he'd been in a crowded airport and the next there was only him and some woman looking back at him from across the terminal. Voices muted and sound ceased and everyone else disappeared. It had happened to Noah yesterday near the Johnny Appleseed sculpture. He felt the same way all over again.

Lacey wore blue jeans, sandals and a gray knit top that fit her perfectly. Her hair was mussed, her eyes as blue as the morning, her nose pert.

He wanted to walk across the room and take her hand, just her hand, and maybe sit with her and talk.

"She's suspicious of my car parked around the corner. I'm pretty sure she was trying to get a make on me while I was getting one on her."

Oh. The P.I. was still talking. Noah came out of his trance with a start.

"She's acting nervous. People who act nervous usually have a reason," Sam said. "If I get any closer she's liable to call the cops. She's camera-shy and she's flighty."

"Is everything okay?" Lacey whispered from the doorway.

Reed motioned her in, quietly saying, "Our private investigator has a lead on Julia."

"Who's there?" Sam asked.

Lacey's eyes widened. She looked at the phone on the desk and said, "I'm the nanny."

"Maybe you want to take me off speaker-phone."

Lacey took the hint and started to leave the room.

"Lacey, wait," Noah said. "She's a friend of the family, Sam."

"And completely trustworthy," Reed added.

"Completely." This, from Marsh.

"You aren't going to believe this," Sam said. "A moving van just pulled into the driveway."

"What does that mean?" Marsh blurted.

"It would appear that she isn't planning to stick around."

Suddenly all eyes were on Marsh. He'd paled beneath his tan. His jaw was set, his lips drawn into a thin line. He looked more haggard suddenly, and a little desperate.

Sam persisted. "I can continue my surveillance then follow the moving van. If she drives her own car and takes a different route I'll have a decision to make. Or—" Sam thought for a moment. "Noah, is your plane flight-ready?"

It was Noah's turn to pale. He had a clear-cut plan in mind for today. And it didn't include flying to Charleston. Half a dozen expletives ran through his head. He glanced at Reed, at Marsh, at Joey and finally at Lacey. He only hoped she would understand.

"Mine's still missing a propeller, Sam, but I'll borrow a plane." He looked at his watch. "I can have Marsh in Charleston in three-and-a-half hours. Four hours, tops."

Marsh was already moving toward the door. He stopped suddenly and looked at the baby, obviously torn.

Lacey took charge with quiet authority. Laying a gentling hand on his arm, she said, "Aren't you glad you hired a nanny? I'll take good care of Joey. Go, both of you, before those movers get Julia's things boxed up and she disappears."

Noah opened his phone and touched the screen. Tom Bender answered on the fourth ring. Still on speakerphone, Sam rattled off a house number and street address, and told them how to avoid the construction on Highway 79. Placing the baby to his shoulder as if he'd been doing it all his life, Reed wrote the information on a notepad in his meticulous handwriting.

Lacey stepped out of Marsh's way. After Sam told them which airport was closest to his stake-out and the make and model of a rental car that would be waiting, Marsh turned around again and said, "Just don't lose her, Sam."

The gravity of the situation stopped everyone at once. Four hours from now they might very well have the answers they were seeking. In four hours they should know if this Julia was the right Julia, and if she'd left Joey on their doorstep three days ago. They might even know why.

As quickly as it had ceased, activity resumed. Sam promised to be in contact, then promptly broke the connection. Marsh went upstairs to get his wallet and change his shoes. Reed of-fered Joey the rest of his formula. And Noah followed Lacey into the living room. He didn't have much more than a minute and he planned to make the most of it.

"This," he said firmly, "has nothing to do with our new beginning."

She looked up at him and whispered, "Did you see the expression on Marsh's face?"

He nodded. Marsh was hurting. The man was pining for this Julia. Until Joey had arrived, Noah hadn't even known Marsh had spent a week on the coast with anyone special.

He glanced into Reed's office again. His fair-haired brother was quietly watching Joey drink his bottle. Had it not been for Joey's arrival, Noah might never have known that he wasn't the only Sullivan with a little bit of rascal running through his veins. That baby was teaching them all so much. And Joey hadn't said a word.

"You take care of Marsh," Lacey told Noah softly. "And I'll take care of Reed and Joey."

Noah's chest expanded, but before he could do more than nod at Lacey, Marsh's footsteps sounded on the stairs. He wished he had time to tell her what he'd been rehearsing since he'd left her in the alley last night. There was just no time for that now.

"It's at least a three-and-a-half-hour flight there and another three-and-a-half hours back," he said. "Allowing for driving time and surveillance time, it'll be at least six o'clock before I return. I'm afraid the next step of our new beginning will have to wait to begin until then."

"The next step?" she asked.

He nodded. The first step had begun before he'd realized what was happening. It had been a culmination of everything that had happened from the moment he'd heard that Lacey was back in Orchard Hill to the moment he'd held her face between his hands and kissed her gently last night. The only part of step one he'd planned had been that kiss. Steps two and three would be different. After all, it wasn't every day that a man got a second chance with a woman like Lacey Bell. "It's a three-step plan. I would tell you but I don't want to spoil the surprise." He smiled and watched the effect it had on her.

Her eyebrows went up in perfect arches and that attitude of hers showed in the tilt of her head. "The sooner you get going, the sooner you can put your money where your mouth is, flyboy."

There was only one place he wanted to put his mouth. Or maybe two. Or three. Hell, he could think of a dozen, all of them soft and lush and—he didn't even try to hide his groan of frustration.

Marsh joined them in the living room and Reed came out of his office with Joey, an empty bottle and the notepad containing the information Sam had given them in his hand. The next few minutes were filled with instructions and reminders and calculations and plans. And then Marsh and Noah were pulling out of the driveway and Reed, Joey and Lacey watched from the back porch.

Lacey smiled and waved.

As Noah sped away, he wondered if she had

any idea what that smile had done to him. He faced the fact that she wasn't simply in his blood.

He'd known her well for ten years. He'd liked her from the beginning. He'd wanted her, and he supposed in his own way he'd loved her for most of that time.

This morning something had changed. He didn't know how it had happened, or why, but he'd seen her standing in the doorway of Reed's office, and he fell headfirst, headlong, head over heels for her. Now he had a burning need to move to step two in his plan.

He rolled down his window. With the warm air rushing over him, he glanced at Marsh. His older brother was staring straight ahead. His arms were folded, his jaw set. Noah wasn't the only one with a burning need.

He checked for traffic and stepped on the gas. His truck shot forward. In a matter of minutes they arrived at the county airfield. Digger was already fueling Tom's twin-engine plane. It was time to get this show on the road or, in this case, in the air.

In the kitchen, Lacey poured two cups of coffee and carried them to the table. Since Reed didn't appear to be ready to relinquish Joey, she moved the child-care book aside and gestured for him to have a seat at a right angle to her. With her pen poised over a yellow legal pad, she said, "I thought we could go over my duties."

Silence.

She looked up from her blank sheet of paper and saw that Reed was staring down at Joey, seemingly lost in thought. This wasn't easy for him. She put her pen down and reached for her camera. Reed seemed oblivious as she removed the lens cap and adjusted the focus. The flash got his attention. As he looked up, she said, "What you're doing for Joey—what all three of you are doing—is a kind of good we don't see very often, Reed. I'm not sure there are three brothers alive who would have handled the situation half as well. That little boy has wrapped his hand around your hearts."

She caught him looking at his wristwatch. He was probably wondering if Noah and Marsh had taken off yet, as she was. She hoped they discovered Joey's mother's identity soon. She remembered an old Bible story about a baby claimed by two mothers. The king's solution was to cut the baby in half. She forgot how it ended, but shuddered at the thought.

She only hoped this situation didn't slice Marsh and Reed apart. "What time is your meeting?" she asked.

At his look of surprise, she motioned to his clothes. The man was dressed to the nines in tan slacks, shoes by a maker she couldn't pronounce, a sky-blue shirt and a striped tie. "Not even *you* wear a tie around home," she said, tongue-in-cheek.

There was something about the look he gave her that reminded her of Noah. It endeared him to her and reminded her that there was more to him than confidence and a keen mind.

"My lawyer and I and two other orchard owners are going to crash a little party this morning," he said. "There's a shady developer from downstate who's proposing the construction of a housing development on Orchard Highway. He's packaging it nice and pretty, but in reality it would be a glorified trailer park. There's a county ordinance a mile high and just as wide against such ventures. But you know how visions of tax revenue can dance in the heads of township and county officials. We're going to make sure no loopholes are created. Luckily, my new brother-in-law got wind of it, and told me before it was too late."

"Your brother-in-law's name is Riley Merrick, isn't it? I heard Madeline got married," Lacey said.

Madeline Sullivan had been a grade behind Lacey in school. Blonde and blue-eyed like Reed, she'd had more than her share of sadness in her life. Recently, she and her new husband had moved to Traverse City and were happily expecting their first child.

"What did Madeline say when you told her about Joey?" she asked.

Reed Sullivan had been the valedictorian of his graduating class and the president of the debate team at Purdue. If he put his mind to it, the man could have won an argument with the devil, yet this innocent question seemed to have struck him dumb. Obviously, he and his brothers hadn't thought to call their sister.

Lacey held her hands out for Joey. While she settled the baby into the crook of her arm, Reed glanced at his watch again.

"Madeline is going to have our hides," he said. "There's no sense calling her now until after we hear from Marsh and Noah."

With that decision made, he began to tell her about Joey's quirks, his likes and his dislikes, how often he ate and how much, and how he liked the new mobile on his crib and didn't like to sleep on his stomach. She jotted everything down with her free hand.

"According to this book written by a group of renowned pediatricians, babies need something called tummy time. I'll work on that. What about baths?" she asked.

Reed did a double take all over again. Evidently, giving the baby a bath hadn't occurred to them yet.

She wrote *BATH* at the top of the page. She and Reed discussed other responsibilities, such as washing baby bottles and folding Joey's laundry. When they were both satisfied that they'd covered everything, she pushed the wrapped package toward him.

"This is for all of you," she said. "Go ahead and open it. While you do that, I think this little guy needs his diaper changed."

"Lacey?" he said when she'd reached the doorway. "A word of caution. The kid's got an aim on him you wouldn't believe."

Reed tore into the wrapping paper. Rather

than ask him to explain, she carried Joey into the room they'd converted into a nursery.

Wow, she thought, turning in a circle. The boys had been busy. A baby crib was in the corner where Marsh's leather sofa had been, a matching changing table and dresser opposite it where a television had been perpetually tuned to the weather. Bright-colored artwork of zoo animals hung on the walls.

She placed Joey on the new changing table and delighted in the way he stared up at her and grinned. Although something drastic must have happened to cause his mother to leave him the way she did, he seemed healthy and content and incredibly adaptable.

She unsnapped his little sleeper and removed his wet diaper. Keeping one hand on his tummy, she reached onto a low shelf for a dry disposable diaper. A fountain sprang forth, dousing everything in its path. She scrambled for the first thing she could find and threw a receiving blanket over the stream.

So that was what Reed had been talking about. A movement at the doorway caught her eye. Reed was there. He held the photograph of Joey she'd developed, framed and wrapped in tissue paper late last night. There was a smile on his face.

The shortest-running temp job she'd ever held in Chicago had lasted three days. During those three days she'd adjusted lighting and backdrops for a photographer taking pictures of men flexing and posing for a fundraising calendar. Reed Sullivan would have been a shoo-in for Mr. July, and yet there was no pounding of her heart or fluttering of butterfly wings. There was only sweet affection.

"It looks like you have everything covered," he said.

She shot him a look she often shot Noah.

Unscathed, he said, "I'm leaving now." He entered the room and strode directly to Joey. "You be good for your Aunt Lacey, all right, buddy?"

Tears sprang to Lacey's eyes. *Aunt* Lacey. How could something so simple fill her with so much wonder?

"I wrote my cell number on that legal pad on the kitchen table," Reed said, apparently oblivious to the fact that he'd just paid her the highest compliment in the world. "Call me if you have any questions or need anything. Anything at all."

"What time do you expect we'll hear from Marsh and Noah?" she asked, still a little awestruck.

"They'll call as soon as they know something," he said.

They both dreaded the wait.

Reed left for his meeting. And Lacey gave Joey his first bath since arriving on the Sullivans' porch. It took an unbelievably long time. Wet babies were slippery and she had only watched April bathe her twins. Joey wasn't the only one soaking wet when it was over. He wasn't the only one enjoying himself, either.

She powdered him and dressed him in a little pair of pants with paw prints on the seat and a T-shirt with a puppy's face on the chest. She read him a story from one of the early-child-hood-development library books she'd brought along. When the baby fell asleep for his morning nap, she laid him in his crib, turned the wireless monitor on and left the nursery.

She tackled the sink full of baby bottles, lids and nipples and folded the baby clothes somebody had piled on the table. The phone rang every half hour. It was Reed every time.

Marsh and Noah hadn't called. She could only imagine what was happening on that tree-lined street in Charleston.

The twin-engine Gulfstream Commander shimmied slightly on a patch of rough air. Marsh put his hand over the pit of his stomach and Noah put both hands on the controls. He pushed the throttle forward and pulled back on the yoke, leveling the airplane out. Shaking his hand slightly once the ride was smooth again, Marsh carefully laid it back on the ice pack in his lap.

Noah kept his expression carefully schooled as he flipped switches and checked dials on the dash. He responded to Air Traffic Control and climbed to three thousand feet as soon as he was cleared by the tower. Now that they were safely above the thunderstorm rolling across Fort Wayne, he pointed the nose due north. From there it was smooth sailing.

They were going home.

The cockpit was drafty and noisy. That wasn't the reason he and Marsh had barely spoken since takeoff. Everything that had happened during the hour they'd been on the ground in Charleston spoke for itself.

The moving van had been in the driveway when they'd pulled up in the rented car. Marsh had parked a few spaces behind Sam's nondescript sedan just as the movers closed the doors. Julia hadn't shown her face, but the movers were getting ready to drive away. While there was still time, it was decided that Noah and Marsh would knock on the bungalow's front door.

The air smelled like honeysuckle and was so heavy with humidity that sweat trickled down both their faces as they approached the house. Marsh rang the doorbell. He was going to do the talking. Noah was along for moral support.

The door opened, but instead of the brown-haired woman they were expecting, a man as big as an ox told them to get the hell off his stoop. His head was shaved, his chest broad, his arms meaty and heavily tattooed.

Marsh, being an all-around decent guy, said, "Hello. I'm an old friend of Julia's. Is she here by any chance?"

"Who wants to know?"

"Tell her it's Marsh Sullivan."

The other man started to turn around, as if he intended to speak to someone over his shoulder. Marsh made the mistake of taking his eyes off him. Noah saw the swing coming and ducked, but Marsh wasn't so lucky. The big man's fist made a resounding whack when it connected with Marsh's jaw.

"Okay, okay," Noah had said, holding up both hands. "We obviously have the wrong house. We're leaving now."

Oxman glanced menacingly at Noah. Marsh used the momentary distraction to slam his fist into the other man's gut. Noah hadn't been trying to create a diversion at all. Not that he blamed Marsh for retaliating. That sucker punch his poor brother had taken had been low-down and dirty. Noah only hoped the grinding he'd heard when Marsh had given the jerk a taste of his own medicine wasn't the bones in Marsh's hand crumbling.

He managed to drag Marsh off the stoop and back to their rental car without either of them losing life or limb. Marsh was swearing a blue streak and both were sweating profusely.

Strangely, Sam wasn't in his car when they got there. They looked all around, but there was no sign of him. They decided to wait inside the car just in case they needed to make a quick getaway.

Sam returned a few minutes later, in worse shape than Marsh. Blood trickled down the side of his cheek and there were bits of leaves and grass on the seat of his pants and in his hair.

Sam Lafferty was in his late thirties. He stood six-four and weighed over two hundred pounds. He worked out every day and it showed. With a groan, he climbed into the backseat.

"What happened to you?" Noah asked.

Sam ran his finger along the screen of a small phone that looked as if it had the capability to launch missiles from outer space while making him a sandwich. Holding the gadget out to Marsh, he said, "I got that picture of her from the front you wanted."

It was actually a video and starred the woman they'd seen in the photographs on Reed's computer back in Orchard Hill over four hours earlier. Sam had caught her slipping out her back door. Noah could tell that she wasn't pleased he was there. There was no sound, but those lips were easy to read.

The last they saw of her in the video, she was performing a high kick that would have made Bruce Lee proud. After that there was nothing but blue sky.

Marsh handed the phone back to the private investigator. Cradling his hand again, he said, "That's not her."

"You're sure?" Sam asked.

"Positive. She's not the woman I knew. She's not even close."

That was that.

It was discouraging, but the beatings Marsh and Sam had taken hadn't been for nothing. One Julia Monroe down, several more to go. Sam was going to continue looking. He would broaden his search for Julia to the Deep South. He was also going to Texas where Reed had spent a night with a stacked blond waitress named Cookie.

Noah had driven back to the airport in Charleston. They'd turned in the rental car and now they were almost home.

Other than a little air turbulence and cabin noise, the trip back had been uneventful. The Gulfstream Commander was Tom Bender's oldest and fastest plane. It was a thrill to fly her. There wasn't anything about flying that wasn't thrilling. Noah liked holding the control loosely in his hands, and was always invigorated by the sensation of gliding a thousand feet above the ground. And yet today, he could hardly wait to land.

"Look!" Marsh said loud enough to be heard over the engine noise and air leaks in the cabin. "There's the orchard. I'd forgotten what it looks like from the air."

There it was, rows of apple trees with bright green leaves, two-track trails running between them. The metal roof on the cider house glowed like melted copper in the bright sunshine. The sprawling house with its peaks and gables and three chimneys sat away from the other buildings. Noah buzzed it the way he always did when he was coming home.

Reed and Lacey rushed outside. He saw Lacey turn Joey around as she pointed at the airplane.

If Noah could have landed in the clearing they used as a parking lot every autumn, he would have. That was how impatient he was to introduce Lacey to the second step in his master plan. He made do with tipping his wing hello.

He didn't know how long step two would last. Part of him hoped to high heaven it didn't take long. It would take as long as it needed to take. He'd rushed her ten years ago. This time, he was going to take it nice and slow.

He was almost sure she was going to give him this chance to begin anew. Only a fool would waste it.

Lacey and Reed both lifted a hand in greeting. Marsh waved back. "Noah?" he called over the cabin noise.

"Yeah?"

"In case I forget later. Thanks."

"Anytime, buddy," Noah said, his chest expanding. "Anytime."

Marsh was going home to the apple trees he'd nurtured, many of them patiently grafted with his own two hands, and the baby he hoped was his son. Noah was flying home to one very special woman.

He banked hard and turned the plane around. The instant they were headed in the right direction, he poured it on. After all, it wasn't every day a man realized that soaring through the wild blue yonder was nothing compared to the thrill of landing in the arms of the woman waiting for him on the ground.

Chapter Seven

At the end of Lacey's first day as Joey's nanny, she left him in Reed's care and, with her library books under one arm and her purse over her shoulder, walked out the back door. She was surprised to see Marsh walking toward her. She'd known that he and Noah were back when they'd buzzed the house, but she hadn't heard anyone drive in.

"I'll see you on Monday," Marsh said gruffly as he walked past. Lacey and Reed had discussed her work schedule, and since the brothers apparently had been in contact and agreed that they would handle Joey's care over the weekend, Lacey saw no reason to detain Marsh now. Cradling his right hand, he went inside without saying another word.

Noah was waiting for her in the driveway. Unlike Marsh, he looked relaxed and at ease. "Hey, Lace," he said. "Got a minute?" His voice had taken on a sleepy velvet smoothness that didn't necessarily mean he was sleepy.

Shading her eyes with one hand, she was pretty sure she was about to hear about step two. They seemed to have the same idea at the same time and, in unison, cut across the driveway to the shade of an enormous maple tree. An old-fashioned swing hung from a high branch. After giving the ropes a tug, Noah said, "Care for a push?"

She hadn't expected that, but she set her things out of the way and tested the ropes, too. "Maybe a small one."

He slipped silently behind her, and then she

felt herself being drawn backward. With a whoosh, she was soaring through the balmy evening air. A little giggle bubbled out of her.

"Want another?" he asked.

"No." She laughed out loud. "This was easier on my stomach when I was a kid."

"Do you remember the first time we went out, Lacey?"

"Out?"

"You know, on our first date."

She glanced over her shoulder at him to see if he was serious. His eyes, those deep brown eyes, were trained on hers. His lips were parted slightly, the edges tilted up just enough to tell her it was an honest question.

She straightened her arms and leaned back. Her hair nearly brushing the grass every time she passed the middle, she looked up at the branches disappearing in the lacy green leaves and considered Noah's question.

Back in school, he was one of those guys all the girls noticed. Two grades ahead of her, he'd driven an old white Charger, a sweet car if there ever was one, until he wrapped it around a tree his senior year. How he made it out alive was anybody's guess. He'd been popular with everybody, even the teachers who shook their heads and threw their hands up in surrender for all the times he pushed his limits and theirs.

Lacey's path didn't cross his until a few years later. He'd grown up a little by then. He hadn't settled down, but he'd found something he loved more than driving too fast and raising hell.

Late one night after he'd returned from a vigorous yearlong Airfield Operations Specialist training program down in Florida, she stepped onto the landing hoping to catch a little relief from the sweltering August heat. What she'd caught was Noah Sullivan's attention as he was cutting through the alley. To this day she remembered the butterflies that had fluttered inside her rib cage when he'd looked up at her and said, "Hey."

She'd stared down at him from the top of those

steps. She might have smiled but she didn't say a word.

"Are you coming down here?" he'd asked.

Raised over the local bar, she'd learned how to take care of herself. She'd taken plenty of risks, but she didn't take chances with guys in dark alleys, no matter how cute they were. "I'm not planning to."

He'd laughed. And she was smitten.

"Mind if I sit down here, then?" he asked.

"Suit yourself."

He made himself comfortable on the third step from the bottom. After a while she'd settled on the top step. They'd talked for two hours, him looking up, and her looking down, cigarette smoke and noise wafting into the alley every time one of her dad's customers opened the tavern's back door. When Noah returned the next night, he moved up a few steps, and she moved down. Before long, they sat in the middle, side by side.

A few weeks later he took a job flying wealthy

businessmen from one corner of Texas to the other. The next time she saw him she was nineteen and he was twenty-one. He came into The Hill where she'd worked as a waitress. Her shift was just ending, so she'd taken off her apron and he'd walked her home. Again, they'd wound up talking for hours. He flew off into the wild blue yonder often during the next few years, but he always came back to her.

Now he was asking if she remembered their first date. She hopped off the swing and faced him. Slipping her hands into the front pockets of her jeans, she said, "Did we go to the movies?"

"The first movie we saw was about a group of World War II fighter pilots. We walked to the Division Street Theater and you paid your own way. Not a date in my book."

"Did we go for a drive or grab a burger somewhere?"

"That doesn't count as a date, either."

"I guess I don't remember our first date," she said.

He smiled, and her heart turned over. "That's because we never went on a first date." He came closer, the swing still rocking gently between them. "All those years we did just about everything else. How could I have missed that?"

She didn't have anything to say to that.

A warm breeze ruffled his shaggy hair and fluttered the hem of her gray shirt. A car drove by, loud music blasting from its open windows. When only the vibration of the bass remained, Noah said, "Would you have dinner with me, Lacey?"

"Dinner?" Okay, she really needed to stop repeating everything he said.

His throat convulsed on a swallow. She realized this was important to him. "Yes," he said, "dinner. You and me in a restaurant that uses cloth napkins. If you say yes, it'll be our first date."

"When were you thinking we would go on this first date?"

"How about right now?" His voice had deepened again, stirring her in a way no other man ever had.

Glancing down at her clothes, she said, "I'm not dressed for dinner at a restaurant that uses cloth napkins."

"How long would it take you to get ready? An hour?" He must have interpreted the look she shot him, because he slanted her a smile he didn't overuse. "An hour and a half, then?"

There were a dozen reasons—all of them good—why she should ignore the way her heart rose up like a ballerina on tiptoe, ready to start twirling. There was only one reason she didn't, and it had everything to do with the promise in Noah's smile.

"An hour and a half, it is," she said, surprised at how cool, calm and collected she sounded. She picked up her purse and camera and books and started across the grass.

She felt his eyes on her as she opened her car door and got in. Finding her keys in the bottom of her bag, she stuck them in the ignition. *Oh-my-gosh-oh-my-gosh-oh-my-gosh.* As she drove out of sight, excitement erupted in a screech of laughter. She cranked the radio up and crested a hill, once again leaving her stomach behind.

She kept to the speed limit, but it wasn't easy. She made a left turn on Elm and then made a beeline for Baldwin Street. She had April on the phone when she pulled into her driveway.

"I need your help," she said, getting out of the car.

April met her at the door. "What's wrong?" she asked, her curly hair in wild disarray.

"I need to borrow a dress."

"A dress?"

Face-to-face but still on the phone, they both burst out laughing. Lacey put her phone away and went in. Being careful not to step on the coloring books and matching pink boas on the living-room floor, she said, "I have a date. A first date."

"Who's here, Mommy?" a little girl called from the next room.

"It's Aunt Lacey," April answered over her shoulder. To Lacey she said, "A date with who?"

Aunt Lacey. She took a moment to savor the sound of it. Her hand settled momentarily on her abdomen. See, she thought, recalling the serious conversation she'd had with her doctor following her second surgery in Chicago. A woman didn't have to *have* children to have children in her life. With a watery smile, she said, "With Noah."

"Follow me." April spun around and led the way across the living room without stepping on a thing.

Jay and April had purchased the house on Baldwin Street shortly after they got married. Built seventy years ago when houses were small and lots were large, it consisted of a living room, an eat-in kitchen and one bathroom with a bedroom on either side. The upstairs had sloping ceilings and walls that were unfinished. It was the first thing Jay was going to do when he came back from Afghanistan. Well, Lacey thought as she followed her petite friend to her bedroom, maybe not the first thing. First, they would begin anew.

There was a lot of that going around.

April didn't ask Lacey if she'd lost her mind. She didn't suggest that going on a first date with Noah now was impossible. She was Lacey's friend, and if Lacey said she needed her help April was going to help her.

She reached to the back of the closet and started flipping through hangers. "This won't do. Neither will this. Or this. What about this?" She held up something only to put it back. "Never mind." Reaching the end, she popped her head out. "A dress, you say."

"Yes."

April looked askance at Lacey for the first time since she'd arrived. "Honey, I don't know how to break this to you, but your chest isn't going to fit into anything I own."

Lacey glanced down at the front of her shirt. Oh, dear. "Noah is picking me up in less than an hour and a half. I don't have time to go to the mall."

The twins came scampering into the room. One had curls like April, the other straight hair like Jay. Both climbed onto their mother's bed.

"No jumping," April warned.

Thwarted, the first plopped down in the middle of the bed and her sister climbed off.

"Wait. I have an idea." April bounded from the room very much the way her daughters had just bounded in. When she returned, she was carrying a garment bag.

Lowering the zipper to reveal the edge of an aqua-colored dress, she said, "I only wore this once. I was still nursing the girls, so I actually had cleavage. Jay couldn't take his eyes off me. Wear it at your own risk."

Lacey drew the dress from the bag. As light as

a feather, it was sleeveless. Since she and April were both a hair under five-five, the length was perfect. The bodice overlapped, forming a V that didn't look too low. The skirt wrapped around, held together with a tie at the side of the waist. Holding the confection in front of her at the mirror, she said, "Are you sure you don't mind loaning it to me?"

"As I said. I wore it when I was nursing, and I'm not planning a repeat performance."

Lacey could feel April watching for her reaction to her inadvertent mention of pregnancy. She'd broken it off with Noah because of her desire to have babies of her own. April knew about Lacey's ruptured appendix and the complications that had followed. But Lacey was starting anew, and that meant growth. It was spontaneous and exciting, the outcome unknown. And this dress was going to be perfect for taking a leap of faith.

"Well, girls?" Lacey said, smiling at April's

adorable children. "Do you think Aunt Lacey will look good in this dress?"

The three-year-olds clapped. And April smiled again. Lacey beamed at all three. *Aunt* Lacey had a certain ring to it.

"What about shoes?" she asked April. "Will my brown sandals do?"

"Trust me, Noah isn't going to be looking at your feet. How much time did you say you have?"

Oh, my. The clock was ticking. Lacey started in one direction, stopped and started again.

"Leave the dress," April commanded. "I'll bring it with me along with everything else we'll need. Go take your shower. Make it a quick one. I'll be a few minutes behind you. Girls, go finish your chicken nuggets. We're going to Aunt Lacey's to help her get ready for her date."

"What's a date?" one of them asked.

At the door Lacey listened for April's reply. "It's like Cinderella's Ball."

"Is Aunt Lacey a princess?"

"Yes, Gracie, she is. And her prince isn't going to know what hit him."

April Avery was helping her twins down the stairs when Noah pulled into the parking space in the alley. He tossed his sunglasses onto the dash of his pickup and got out. Somewhere, the marching band was practicing for the upcoming Fourth of July parade, the drums and occasional trumpet blast carrying on the warm air. Dog walkers were out on Division Street, and two boys were being reprimanded for skateboarding on the sidewalk.

"Whoa. You don't clean up too bad, Noah," April said on her way by.

Noah liked April, and was about to tell her she wasn't so bad herself, but he happened to catch a glimpse of Lacey at the top of the stairs by her door. Whatever he'd been about to say was wiped from his mind.

That glimpse of Lacey had been fleeting, and

yet he started up the stairs like a moth drawn to a flame. At the top, he found her door ajar.

"Lacey?"

Her muffled voice carried from a distant room. "Come in, Noah. I'll be right out. I just have to change purses."

The boxes that had filled the living room several nights ago were gone. There was a slip-cover on the sofa and a small glass that held two dandelions on a table beside it. Propped behind the makeshift vase was a photograph of Joey. There was a similar one in a frame in the living room at home.

"Take your time." He was opening a book from the library when Lacey entered the room.

"Hi," she said.

"Hi." He caught her looking at the flowers in his hand. She caught him looking at her in that dress. The color was somewhere between green and blue. The skirt fluttered like a whisper as she walked closer. The neckline ended at a V that whispered something else entirely.

"At first I wasn't sure how this first-date idea was going to go," she said.

He met her in the middle of the room and handed her the bouquet. The flowers had been an afterthought. Witnessing the pleasure she took in them made him wonder what else he'd left out in the past. "And now?" he asked. "How would you say it's going now?"

"So far so good." It was a phrase he'd heard her use often. She was the same Lacey. Or was she?

Their gazes met, held, slid away and met again, and it felt very much like a first date, full of potential and excitement and discovery. Her hair waved close to her face, the ends resting lightly at the delicate ridges of her collarbones. Her lips were shiny, her cheeks bronzed, but her eyes stole the show. Bluer than blue, they were surrounded by lashes that looked a mile long.

"I would offer you something to drink," she said, "but I only recently moved back in, and I started a new job today, and I'm afraid I haven't had a chance to go to the store."

It was exactly the sort of comment someone would make on a first date. "We can get something to drink at the restaurant," he said. "Do you like Italian food?"

He knew she did. And he knew it was going to be a memorable first date when she burst out laughing. This was Lacey. Only better. He was himself, but he was going to be better, too.

She put the flowers in water and switched on a lamp so she wouldn't come home to the dark. Slipping the purse she'd kept him waiting for over her shoulder, she preceded him out the door.

After she'd buckled her seat belt and he'd buckled his, he said, "I just returned from a little trip myself."

He had her in stitches as he described his and Marsh's encounter with Oxman this afternoon. By the time he'd told her about the size-six shoeprint the wrong Julia Monroe had left on the private investigator's cheek, Noah was laughing, too.

The restaurant he'd chosen was one of those chains that had popped up in college towns throughout the Midwest these past few years. Decorated in faux old-world-Italy style, it wasn't exactly five-star, but Reed had said the food was good, the waitstaff was prompt, and there wasn't a television or a paper napkin in the place.

Since it wasn't the kind of establishment that took reservations, they'd had to wait to be seated. Not long after the hostess led them to a table under a window, their waiter appeared. "Could I interest the two of you in something from the bar?"

Normally Noah's drink requests leaned toward a shot and a beer. Tonight, he ordered a bottle of the house wine, and watched as Lacey turned her attention to her menu. He put his down. He knew what he wanted. He'd already decided what he was going to order, too.

Lacey could feel Noah's gaze on her. Glad to have something to focus on, she continued to peruse the menu, still deciding between the lasagna and the baked chicken. In the back of her mind, she thought April was right. Noah was having trouble keeping his eyes off her in this dress.

April had brought a cache of products with her when she'd arrived. There were potions and lotions, makeup, perfume and jewelry. She'd helped Lacey decide how to wear her hair, and inspected her makeup when Lacey was finished applying it. Lacey had taken April's advice and applied another coat of mascara and a spray of flowery perfume, but she'd decided against wearing a necklace and earrings. The dress was enough.

The waiter arrived with their wine and took their orders. While Noah poured, Lacey studied him unhurriedly. He'd never been pretty-boy handsome, not this man. His features were too rugged to be considered classic. Pretty boys had never appealed to her. Noah had always been a little rough around the edges. Earlier she'd noticed that his belt and shoes were a tad scuffed and his chocolate-brown pants sat just below his waist as if they'd been made for him. The combination of his shaggy hair and tan skin above the open collar of a finely tailored shirt was declaring open season on her senses.

She asked him questions about his work and his travels as if she didn't know him from Adam. And he asked her about hers the same way. Their meals arrived, and they refilled their wineglasses, and they talked about anything and everything under the sun. Much of what they said was simply a refresher course, and, yet, refreshing it was. Somehow it all felt brand-new.

Last night he'd told her they would look back for years to come and remember it as the night they began anew. By the time the waiter brought Noah the check and a take-out box containing the uneaten portion of her entrée, Lacey had already forgotten much of what they'd talked about tonight. It wasn't the conversation that made the night memorable. It was the care Noah took to make sure she had everything she wanted.

She didn't miss the significant look the waiter gave Noah when he took his credit card, or the slight smile Noah gave the young waiter in return. She'd seen that kind of male communication before. It was the equivalent to the beat of distant drums and smoke signals, and it meant *go for it!*

She wasn't certain what Noah was planning, but she could tell what he was thinking by the way his gaze lingered on her mouth, and the base of her neck, and the V of her dress. And knowing sent those butterflies aflutter.

He held the door for her as she got in his truck. Now that the evening was winding down, she rolled her window down and let her hair blow in the onrushing breeze. He rolled his down, too, and to Lacey it felt a little as if they were flying.

Flying would have explained why the drive back to Division Street lasted only as long as a blink of an eye. The mercury lights were on in the alley when they got there. The poles were spaced apart so that each circle of light ended before the next one began. Noah parked between two of them. And for the first time since the date began, they both fell silent.

She looked over at him. The little gash on his lip had healed, and his hair was windblown now, too. He was looking back at her, and it occurred to her that she didn't know how this night would end, not really. It was part of the great unknown. She didn't have to know. Somehow not knowing added to the excitement and the pleasure.

He drew in a deep breath, and said, "I'll walk you to your door."

Her chest filled with wonder. Would their first date really end at her door?

She slipped out on her side and met him at the front of his truck. They took a leisurely walk up the stairs side by side. At the top, she dug through her purse for her key. A tear sheet from a magazine came out with her keys. "I forgot I brought a personality quiz with me."

"A personality quiz?" He took the key from her and put it in the lock.

"I took it myself last night and brought it along in case we ran out of things to talk about during dinner."

He faced her. The dim yellow light beside her door was behind him, casting his shadow on her. His eyes looked darker, his expression difficult to read. "You took it, you said?"

She nodded.

"What did the results say?"

For a moment the heat in his eyes made her forget the question. In a moment or two, he was going to kiss her good-night. She wondered if he had any idea that she'd been waiting for this kiss since he'd arrived.

Sliding the torn pages back into her shoulder bag, she said, "It turns out I'm not a morning person." She hadn't meant it to sound so sultry and sensual.

"I'll take that under advisement." He placed his hands lightly on her shoulders, drawing her closer. Their mouths touched, and it felt like the beginning, like one of those childhood wishes to go back and do something over, only better, knowing now what she didn't know then.

When he'd asked her earlier if she remembered their first date, she'd told him no. If he'd asked if she remembered their first kiss, she would have said yes. It had happened after he'd finished his six-month stint flying wealthy businessmen from one corner of Texas to the other.

There was a balmy breeze tonight, but that night winter had just begun. It was three days before Christmas and it had been snowing since early afternoon. All anybody Lacey had waited on at The Hill had talked about was Christmas. She'd decorated the tree in the restaurant and another one at home, but she really hadn't been looking forward to Christmas that year.

That changed when the door opened just before closing time. The movement set off the jingle of the sleigh bells Rosy Sirrine had fastened over the door the day after Thanksgiving. The sight of Noah Sullivan staring back at her, the collar of his bomber-style winter coat turned up against the weather and snowflakes melting in his dark shaggy hair, had set off another round of chimes in the pit of Lacey's stomach.

She'd exchanged her white apron for her winter coat, and he'd walked her home. And she remembered thinking there was nothing more still or magical than the first measurable December snow. They'd talked all the way to the back alley. She didn't recall the subject matter, but she remembered thinking that Christmas was going to come early for her that year.

And it had.

They'd been young and impetuous and more than a little wild back then. He'd kissed her at the bottom of the stairs. That first kiss had led to another, and another, and had landed them both in her bed.

It was summertime now, and all these years later Noah's kiss wasn't impetuous or wild, as their first kiss had been. Tonight, his kiss was a contradiction and a promise, so deeply etched in her memory it might have been entered in an ancient record and yet so new it seemed to have been invented just for them. Unbelievably intimate, it caused her heart to speed up and her thoughts to slow. It was thunder and lighting and a warm, nourishing rain. If it went on forever, it would be over too soon.

She wasn't sure if she swayed closer or if he did. She only knew that her body came up against his—thighs, hips and bellies. A moan escaped her at the proof of how badly he wanted her.

A groan escaped him, too, but he imposed an iron will upon himself. Drawing away gallantly, but with obvious reluctance, he pressed his forehead to hers for a moment. "Good night, Lacey."

"I had a wonderful time, Noah. I mean that."

He watched her slip out of his arms, and he waited until she'd closed the door before starting down the stairs.

Covering her lips with her fingertips to hold in her cheer, she pressed her back against the door. The lamp she'd left on cast a soft glow through the room. She took a deep breath of air scented of roses and lilies and a handful of other flowers in the bouquet he'd given her. He'd never brought her flowers. As much as she'd loved him, she'd never felt quite like this.

Elation bubbled out of her. She spun away from the door and twirled around and around, her skirt billowing like a dancer's. Stopping when she got dizzy, she stood perfectly still, waiting for the room to stop spinning. She looked around the apartment that once had been cluttered with her dad's things. She was beginning to understand what he'd meant by hidden treasure.

She'd always thought she'd wanted one thing. The night they'd broken up, she'd told Noah she wanted a house with a picket fence and a dog and children. Hiding beneath the surface now was something else.

She might always want babies, but she was starting to realize that she could have a rich and meaningful life without having children of her own. She was Aunt Lacey.

As soon as the tavern sold, she would pay off her medical bills, and she would be free to explore another kind of future. Wasn't that what Noah had wanted?

April was bringing a client to see the tavern tomorrow. Lacey thought for a moment about her Houdini, and wondered where she would go if it sold and a new owner reopened the bar. Again, Lacey wondered about the other woman's identity. She was probably downstairs getting comfortable right now.

The idea piqued her curiosity. *Was* she downstairs right now?

Where did she go during the day? And why had she chosen Bell's Tavern? How on earth was she getting in?

Lacey's silent questions led her to her door.

Opening it an inch at a time, she peered out. She knew every hiding place in the alley. She also knew which window was near the pool table. What if she tiptoed down the stairs and took a little peek inside? It was still her tavern, after all. What harm could there be in slipping into the shadows where the mercury light didn't reach?

She opened her door a little farther. It was midnight. The moon was out, spilling weak silver light onto the stairs. She turned one ear to the night. Voices and music carried from the outdoor tables at the Alibi Bar across Division Street, but the alley itself was quiet.

Lacey slipped out onto the stoop and carefully drew the door shut. She peered down into the shadows. Satisfied that the coast was clear, she tiptoed down the steps. Again, she listened intently. Hearing nothing, she crept silently from shadow to shadow. At the building, she ducked down like a cat burglar and scuttled beneath the first window where the for-sale sign now hung from the inside. Up and down she went until she came to the window in the far corner.

Her heart was racing with excitement now. Rising up on tiptoe, she looked in. Seeing only her own reflection, she pressed her nose closer. She curled her hands beside her eyes like field glasses and leaned all the way to the glass. That was better. She could see one end of the pool table. She inched to the next pane, and studied the patch of moonlight spilling onto the floor. Try as she might, she couldn't make out the sleeping bag underneath. Or wait. Was someone inside?

Her breath caught at the possibility. She had to go up on tiptoe to see better. Nobody was inside, at least nobody she could see. That had obviously been wishful thinking.

She was in the middle of heaving a deep sigh when a hand cupped her shoulder. A big, heavy, strong, terrifying hand.

Her heart reared up and alarm bells clanged in her head. She spun around and opened her mouth to scream.

Chapter Eight

Oh-my-god-oh-my-god-oh-my-god. This was it. The moment every woman feared.

Lacey knew better than to skulk around in dark alleys, even in towns with only 25,000 people. This was the price she paid for throwing caution to the wind. How could she have been so trusting, so stupid? She would probably be murdered, her body never found. Or worse.

She spun around. Fright—stark and vivid—lodged in her throat. She couldn't even scream. Or breathe. Or think.

"It's okay, Lacey, it's me."

She blinked in the darkness. Her heart was racing so fast she thought she'd heard somebody call her by name.

"Are you okay?"

She knew that voice. A man dressed in dark pants and shirt, making him all but invisible, stood a few feet from her. She peered up at him.

Noah?

He wasn't an ax murderer. Or a rapist. Or her Houdini.

It was Noah.

Her heart was racing. It wasn't a good feeling, and it couldn't be good for her. Her hands automatically went to her hips and that fighter's chin of hers went up. "Somebody needs to put a bell on you. You should know better than to scare people like that. What if I had a weapon or a black belt in karate or a bad heart? What are you doing here, anyway?"

He held up the white box from the restaurant. "You left this in my truck." There was an edge of annoyance in his voice, but he continued his explanation. "I was going the wrong direction when I remembered your leftovers. The cop I saw made me think twice about doing a U-turn, so I parked on Division Street and walked over. I think the question should be what the hell are *you* doing out here?"

She ducked her head.

Noah knew that tactic. It was a ruse to buy Lacey some time until she thought of a way to change the subject.

"I forgot all about my doggie bag," she said, gesturing to the square box in his hand. "You didn't have to make a special trip to bring it back. But thank you just the same."

Noah saw through the innocent act like a picture window. He took a step backward, putting a little distance between them. The near-darkness bleached the color out of everything, so that her pale aqua dress looked silver. Her face was pale, too. He couldn't see the expression in her eyes, but they were wide-open. Undeterred, he asked, "Why were you looking in the window?"

"Shh." She glanced over her shoulder. "She'll hear you."

She stopped so quickly he knew she hadn't meant to say that. "Why were you looking in the window?" he said again, intentionally louder.

She covered his mouth with her hand. Making a show of looking all around again, she removed her hand and said, "If I have to tell you I'd rather not do it down here where everybody and anybody might hear."

She didn't exactly stomp her feet, but she didn't make any attempt to be quiet as she led the way up the steps. At the top she opened the door and traipsed on in. She didn't turn around until he'd closed the door firmly behind him.

In no mood to make concessions, he took the leftovers to the kitchen and stuck the foam box in the old refrigerator. After closing the door with a loud clank and making sure the handle was latched, he retraced his steps and found her still standing in the center of the room. Her color was heightened. Her eyes were large and round, her mascara smudged slightly. Something was going on, and he wasn't leaving until he knew what it was.

He folded his arms, waiting.

She raised her big blue eyes to his. She must have realized that he wasn't going anywhere until she told him the truth, because she heaved a great sigh and finally began. "If you must know I was hoping to get a glimpse of Houdini."

It was his turn to do a double take. "I thought Houdini was dead."

"What? Oh. He is."

"Since when do you believe in ghosts?" he asked.

With a roll of her eyes, she said, "Her name isn't really Houdini."

"Whose name?" he asked, louder again.

"Whoever has been sleeping underneath my pool table." She blinked, gnashed her molars together and groaned. Obviously, she hadn't meant to say that, either.

"Somebody has been sleeping under the pool table? Downstairs? In the tavern? Right below you?" His voice grew louder with every question.

She winced. She might say nothing, but she wouldn't lie. He knew from experience that she couldn't help telling the truth, even when it pained her.

"I thought you had the locks changed."

"I did."

"You're telling me somebody is breaking into the tavern? An out-of-business, closed, empty tavern? On a regular basis?" Okay, he admitted that was a little loud, even for him. Toning it down to a less deafening decibel level, he said, "And you thought, what? That you were going to catch him red-handed? You could have been killed. Did you think of that?"

"Actually, I didn't think of that until you showed up."

Failing to see the humor, he reached into his pocket and pulled out his phone. "I'm calling the police."

"Noah, don't."

He'd already pressed the nine and the one.

"I called the police," she said.

He paused, his finger on the final number. "I don't hear any sirens."

"I didn't call them tonight." She huffed as if he was really starting to annoy her. "I called them when I discovered the sleeping bag and water bottle tucked out of sight underneath the pool table."

"When was that?"

She glanced at the clock. "It's after midnight, so I guess technically it was four days ago now."

He remembered how spooked she'd been when he'd caught her unawares down in the bar the other day when he'd come over to apologize for accusing her of deserting Joey. Now he understood why she'd been so nervous. It would have been nice if she had told him then rather than risk her life by herself. But, of course, she wouldn't have told him. They hadn't been a couple then.

He had every intention of rectifying that, but first he was going to get to the bottom of this. He widened his stance a little and put his hands on his hips again. "What did the police say?"

"Maybe we should sit down."

Obviously, this wasn't going to be a short story. He glanced at his two options and chose the old leather recliner. He sank deep into the cushion. Rather than sit back, he leaned forward, his knees apart, his elbows resting on his thighs.

Lacey lowered herself daintily to the sofa adjacent to him. "Perhaps I should start at the beginning." She sat forward, too, her knees together beneath her skirt, her hands clasped. "The other day I was showing April through the tavern. She was taking measurements for the listing and I happened to notice a cue stick lying out. Then I saw something sticking out from underneath the pool table. It was a sleeping bag. I knew it hadn't been there when I swept the day before."

"So you called the police."

She nodded. "They sent a seasoned officer who checked all the windows and doors and locks. Everything was buttoned up nice and tight. Since the sleeping bag was narrow and on the feminine side, he said it was probably some young high-school or college student or maybe a runaway just passing through town. He was pretty sure she wouldn't be back."

Noah took an easier breath.

Lacey ruined that when she said, "But then yesterday I found a partially eaten bag of mixed nuts, and the water bottle had been replaced with a bottle of green tea."

He sat up straighter. Something about this bothered the back of his mind. Hell, everything about this bothered the back of his mind.

"I still don't know how she's getting in and out—that's why I call her Houdini," Lacey said.

"I'm pretty sure Officer Pratt was right about her gender because there was a pink lipstick print on her water bottle and she has long brown hair."

"You've seen her?" he asked.

She shook her head once. "I found a strand of her hair on the sleeping bag last night."

He stood. "Get your things together."

"What?" She rose, too. "What things?"

"A suitcase. With a change of clothes and whatever else you need. You're staying with us."

"Noah, I'm not packing my suitcase." He opened his mouth, but before he could tell her she sure as hell was, she said, "I'm not going anywhere."

"Somebody is living in the bar. It could be anybody. A vagrant. A murderer. A lunatic. A serial killer."

"She's not a murderer or a lunatic or a serial killer."

"You don't know that. And if this person can

get around the locks downstairs, she could get in up here. Pack your things."

The only move she made was to dig in her heels.

"Why are you arguing?" he demanded, turning toward her.

"I'm not arguing."

"You're right," he said impatiently. "You're flat-out refusing to see reason."

"Where is the reason? Noah, I spent my formative years in this apartment. There were far scarier people than this girl walking by at all hours of the night, shattering beer bottles, howling at the moon. Why are you worried now?"

He clamped his mouth shut so hard she probably heard it. He hated that she was right. Nobody liked to be wrong, but in this instance it was worse because it reminded him of how much he'd taken for granted.

Why was he worried now? A better question would have been why hadn't he worried about her back then? He should have been scared out of his mind. Her dad had spent every night behind the bar serving drinks to his customers. Lacey could have gone anywhere and done anything, and often did. And yet Noah hadn't experienced this brand of fear until now. It was a direct result of that headlong, head-over-heels tumble he felt himself taking for her.

"I don't want anything bad to happen to you, all right?" he said.

She smiled. And he wanted to bite through his cheek.

His groan had a lot in common with a growl. He put both hands on his head, and stood looking at her, his elbows akimbo and his hair sticking out. "Why do you want to stay here when you know somebody is breaking in and out of a locked building?"

"Because I'm not afraid."

"You're not afraid." He let his hands fall to his sides.

"There," she said, tipping her head ever so much. "See? I knew you would understand."

"You're not afraid."

Her smile brightened. "I haven't been afraid all night."

Noah faced the fact that Lacey wasn't talking about things that went bump in the dark or this mysterious Houdini wannabe anymore. She wasn't *afraid* of what was happening between them. Damn this burgeoning admiration.

Then and there he wanted to swing her into his arms and carry her to bed. He'd start by untying the sash at the side of her waist of that amazing blue-green concoction she was wearing, and then he'd move to the straps at her shoulders. He would take his time there; he would take his time everywhere.

"But if it'll make you feel better," she said, "there is one thing I'd be willing to do."

Only one? he thought. "There is?" he asked. "And what's that?"

"I could give you my phone number if you'd like. If it isn't too forward of me after only the first date."

"You're something else, do you know that?" he asked.

"Are you just figuring that out?"

She had him there.

She recited her phone number as she walked to the door. She opened it and held it. Saying nothing, she waited for him to take the hint. Hitting him over the head with a two-by-four would have been a hint. This was less subtle.

For a split second he considered grasping her hand and pulling her out onto the stoop with him. Keeping her firmly at his side, he would proclaim to the world that Lacey Bell was his.

But that was part of step three. He couldn't take that leap just yet. He owed her a courtship, dammit, so he walked out the door she was holding open. Over his shoulder, he said, "Lock that. Wedge a chair under the damn doorknob, too."

"I will, but only because I know it'll make you feel better."

On his way to his parked truck on Division

Street, hc looked back. Her door was closed. In his mind's eye he saw her dragging a chair from the kitchen and wedging it beneath the doorknob. She'd said she would, and she didn't lie.

He met two groups of people taking a short-cut through the alley. The first looked like a couple of old army buddies. The second was a man and woman he'd seen having drinks at the outside tables in front of the Alibi across the way. Nobody had long brown hair.

Long brown hair.

He'd lost track of how many times that de-scription had come up in less than twenty-four hours. Marsh said his Julia had had long brown hair when he'd known her. And Lacey believed her intruder had long brown hair, too. Was there a connection they were all missing?

Four days ago Lacey had noticed the sleeping bag under the pool table for the first time. The night before that somebody had left Joey on the

Sullivans' porch. Now Noah wondered if it was the same woman.

That would be the mother of all coincidences, but it didn't explain how Lacey's Houdini was getting in, or why. And if she were Marsh's Julia, why would she leave the baby with them and then stay nearby in a deserted tavern? There were a dozen whys, and just as many ifs, ands and buts. It was enough to make his head pound.

Noah dug his keys out of his pocket and started his truck. At the red light he pulled his phone out, too. He slid it open and deftly pressed the number from memory. Before the light turned green, he broke the golden rule of first dates.

"I have an idea," he said after Lacey answered.

He hadn't waited twenty-four hours to call. He hadn't even waited until he got home. That was a no-no.

"What kind of idea?" He heard the smile in her voice.

"For our second date," he said. No-no number two—never assume.

"What did you have in mind?" Had her voice always been so sultry and deep?

"Have you ever been on a stakeout?" he asked.

"Oh, Noah, that's a great idea. It so happens I know the perfect place."

"I figured you would. I'm going to call Sam tomorrow and get a few pointers. I'll call you then."

She disconnected first, but not before he heard her little gleeful giggle. Noah was shaking his head when he hung up. If anybody had been looking they would have seen that he was smiling, too.

"Today might need to be reclassified," Noah said.

Something told Lacey that Noah wasn't referring to the fact that Marsh and Reed had decided they didn't need the services of a temporary nanny on the weekend and therefore she had the day off. One hand at the small of her back, she went around to the other side of the old whiskey barrel she was filling with petunias and waited for Noah to make his point. Ultimately, his silence drew her gaze.

Bent at the waist, he stood on the fourth step from the bottom of the staircase leading to her apartment. He had a wide paintbrush in his hand. A gallon of gray paint sat on another step.

Lacey had never been accused of being particularly patient, but in this case the view gave her plenty to appreciate while she waited for him to continue. His jeans were faded, his legs long, his backside just muscular enough to be interesting. The temperature had reached eighty-six degrees today. Here in the alley the bricks and the blacktop had soaked up the heat until it felt like at least a hundred. There hadn't been more than a whisper of a breeze all evening. Noah had shed his shirt an hour ago before the sun sailed out of sight behind the tall buildings on the opposite side of the alley.

He finished painting another step, then slowly straightened up. Making a show of stretching, he cast a casual glance over his shoulder as a group of people strolled past. Lacey saw them, too. There were three men, all of them balding, and four women, all with short hair. Like everyone else who'd taken this shortcut to the Orchard Hill Theater's grand reopening a few blocks away, they seemed to have no idea that the painting and flower-planting was a cover for the stakeout Lacey and Noah were conducting.

Going down another step, Noah dipped his paintbrush in the can again. "I don't think there are two other people in the world who've had a second date like this."

So that's what he'd meant by *reclassification.* Stepping back to view the barrel now filled with yellow, lavender and white flowers next to the stairs, Lacey said, "When we first moved to Orchard Hill, these steps were open. For my fourteenth birthday I asked my dad to install the boards on the back so I wouldn't be terrified that somebody was going to grab my ankle every time I went up or down."

She found herself looking at her pointer finger poking through the hole in the end of the brand-new garden glove she'd found in the clearance bin, remembering the young girl she'd been at fourteen. "Dad bought the lumber that very day. For my birthday a week later he converted the hall closet into a darkroom. I got a decorated cake and a new camera, too."

Finding Noah still looking at her, she smiled.

"Never let it be said I don't know how to work the system."

"You're saying you don't mind this so-called date?" He gestured to their tasks, to the alley setting and the lack of privacy.

"Mind? This is the most fun I've ever had on a second date. And those steps look fantastic. April was right. A coat of paint on the stairs and these flowers next to them really helps to make the entrance to the apartment look more inviting. Hopefully, buyers will agree."

"I thought you might reconsider selling and

reopen the bar," he said, moving down yet another step.

She shook her head. "That would take money. Besides, if I could be anything in the world, I wouldn't be a barkeep."

Noah resumed painting. Noticing the play of light where the sky met the roof of the building on the opposite side of the alley, she automatically reached for her camera. She set the focus then snapped a picture. Next a petunia just opening in the whiskey barrel caught her eye. She took a close-up of it, her garden glove now lying next to it. Through her lens she discovered a ladybug she hadn't noticed before.

She was still taking pictures when Noah finished painting the last step. "Are you hungry?" he asked.

"Starving," she said, snapping a picture of him, too.

"Pizza?"

They'd been taking turns going after something one or the other of them needed. When

Noah ran out of paint, she'd gone to the hardware store for another gallon, leaving him to keep watch in the alley. When she'd needed more potting soil, he'd gone and she'd stayed behind.

"It's my turn," she said. "I need to wash my hands before I go." She was looking at the soil on the tip of her pointer finger, and might have started up the freshly painted steps if Noah hadn't pulled her back.

Since she couldn't very well go out for food without washing her hands, she said, "Maybe you could go pick up a pizza."

She followed the course of his gaze to the black T-shirt draped over the railing at the top. Until the paint dried, he couldn't retrieve his shirt, and without a shirt, he couldn't go into any restaurant in Orchard Hill.

As he extracted his phone from the front pocket of his blue jeans, she took advantage of this legitimate reason to be looking there. When she'd first met him, he'd been thin as a rail. He was one of those guys who would always be lanky, but he'd filled out over the years. His shoulders had broadened and his chest was muscled and accentuated by a spattering of dark curly hair. She glanced away because, well, because this was only their second date for one thing.

Eventually, she noticed that he'd grown silent. It occurred to her that he'd asked her a question. Since he was ordering the pizza, it stood to reason that his question had to do with that. "Surprise me," she said.

And that was exactly what Noah did.

He surprised her when the pizza arrived and he lowered the tailgate on his truck and helped her up as if he were holding her chair in a fine French restaurant. He surprised her when he asked her if she still had that personality quiz she'd mentioned yesterday. After she ran to the cab of his truck where she'd stashed her purse, and brought the tear sheets back with her, he surprised her again and again.

She gave him the quiz between bites of pepperoni-and-mushroom pizza with green peppers and extra cheese. She didn't bother asking him to explain his viewpoint about clowns, but she couldn't help peering over her fountain Coke at him about his latest reply. "Spiders are worse than snakes? Are you kidding me?"

"If I don't answer truthfully I don't see how the results would be accurate," he said.

"Fine. B. Spiders." She circled the corresponding letter. "Even though spiders build incredibly delicate, yet strong—not to mention beautiful—webs out of a substance they produce themselves. Snakes don't build anything."

He shrugged one broad, bare shoulder. If he had issues, his masculinity obviously wasn't one of them. "I think snakes are sexy."

She made a sound of pure disgust. "There is nothing sexy about a snake."

"Tell that to Adam and Eve."

Darkness was falling fast. The mercury lights came on while Lacey's blood was thickening and her thoughts were wandering to naughty scenarios. It was no wonder it took her longer than it should have to calculate his score.

"Am I a night owl, too?" he asked, biting into the last slice.

She carried his total to the results section on the back. She read the short paragraph describing his character type then wadded the paper into a ball. He rescued it from the pizza box and smoothed it out.

Reading the explanation pertaining to his score, he smiled. "I'm morning, noon and night? You don't have to worry about it going to my head." His gaze met hers, and she knew where it was going.

Noah couldn't remember when he'd had this much fun. He admitted that Lacey was right. This may not have been a typical second date, but it was one he would never forget. It wasn't easy to take his eyes off Lacey, and hadn't been since he'd arrived three hours ago. She wore flip-flops and faded cutoffs and a tank top the color of ripe peaches. She'd been wearing a shirt over it when he'd gotten here. It was one of those little feminine numbers, so thin it was practically transparent with pearly buttons and little dots all over it. She'd taken it off about the same time he'd peeled off his T-shirt.

Three teenage girls ran by, giggling. Two of them had long hair. Only one was a brunette and her hair was extremely curly. Lacey and Noah watched them, committing their appearance to memory. So far their stakeout hadn't produced any young women with long, straight brown hair.

When Noah had spoken to Sam on the phone, the P.I. said private investigation work was ninety-eight percent sitting still. "Trust me, the other two percent makes all the boredom worth it."

Noah hadn't been bored. The fact that he'd had fun painting steps was a testament to the company he was keeping.

When they finished eating, he touched the

steps with his fingertips. Deeming them dry, he went up and retrieved his shirt. He pulled it on, then stood looking down at the alley. Lacey was donning her shirt, too.

She'd worn her hair up today, fastened near the top of her head with a shiny clip. As the afternoon turned into evening, more and more tendrils had escaped, curling at her nape and around her ears. Her face was shiny, and there was a smudge of dirt on her shorts. She'd looked beautiful last night in that dress. She looked just as beautiful today.

He started down the steps toward her.

"Is that 'Moon over Miami'?" she called out of the blue.

His attention had been so intent upon her he hadn't noticed the song wafting from a passing radio. Every time a car went by the entrance of the alley, its radio blasting, they'd tried to name the title of the song. It had been Lacey's idea. She could make a game out of anything.

She'd seen their second date's potential from

the beginning. There were so many things he was discovering about her. She'd always been a stickler for washing her hands. Until he'd watched her eat her pizza with a napkin wrapped around her pointer finger, he hadn't realized just how germ-phobic she was.

And she knew something about everything. She was the one who'd told him that new owners were reopening the Orchard Hill Theater. She'd spoken about a grant the city had been awarded for a beautification project that included sprucing up the town's sidewalks, storefronts and alleys.

Noah agreed that the steps looked better with a coat of paint and the flowers, but the real beauty back here was Lacey. There wasn't anything about her he didn't like. Even her stubborn streak was adorable. Marsh and Reed would have called it the blush of a new relationship. In reality, theirs was the blush of an old one.

Gearing up for step three, he met Lacey at the bottom of the stairs, on her way to the trash can underneath them. Since her hands were full of the empty pizza box, napkins and paper drink cups, he went with her and removed the trash can's lid.

"What would you be?" he asked.

She looked up at him in the near darkness, a little furrow forming between her eyes. He wasn't surprised that she had no idea what he was talking about. What surprised him—and humbled him—was that he'd never asked the question before.

"Earlier you said if you could be anything in the world, you *wouldn't* be a barkeep. What would you be?"

He could see the pleasure his interest brought her. Since the clip was sliding from her hair, she whisked it out and shook her hair down. "I would be a professional photographer. I started photography classes in Chicago."

Of course that was what she wanted to be. He remembered the first time he saw her walking to school, her hair short and her jeans tight, a chip on her shoulder and a camera around her neck. She never knew it, but he'd had his eye on her for a long time.

"Now it's your turn," she said. At his blank look, she added, "Tell me something I don't know about you."

From out of the blue, he heard himself say, "My grandfather was a well witcher. And now I think I'd like to kiss you."

When Noah was a kid, he'd seen his grandfather find an underground spring using two divining rods he'd fashioned from pieces of wire. Somehow the electromagnetic field flowing through the water was transmitted up through his grandfather's body and out his hands, causing the rods to cross.

Until Lacey reached up and touched his cheek with the tips of three fingers, slowly letting them trail to his mouth, Noah had never understood the concept of electromagnetism. Her touch changed that. Electricity arced from her body to his, buzzing in places indirectly connected.

"A well witcher, really?" Her smile was sexy as hell. "The kissing part I already knew."

With his heart thundering in his ears and his desire kicking into overdrive, he covered her slender hand with his. Slowly, he dragged it from his lips to his chest. He wanted her to feel what she was doing to his heartbeat before he'd even kissed her.

Her lips parted in the most enticing manner. He swooped down and covered them with his. At that first melding, his heart reared up, then settled into a rhythm that grew stronger with every beat.

The staircase made their little refuge feel secluded. The shadows made it intimate. But it was the touch of his mouth on hers that made it feel like heaven.

Lacey felt Noah's arms come around her, felt herself being drawn up, folded into his embrace.

Heat radiated from the entire length of his body, branding every inch of her body that came into contact with every inch of his.

She went up on tiptoe, diving into a frenzied kiss. She didn't know how he did it, how he made every kiss feel different than the last one. This kiss was rough and possessive, a wild mating of mouths and heat and hunger. As far as second dates went, tonight had been astoundingly wonderful. As far as kisses went, this one was off the charts.

Need shot up between them, the need to open her mouth and deepen the kiss, the need to stroke, retreat and stroke again, the need to look back at where they'd been and look forward to where they might go. More than anything was the need to savor Noah's heat, his passion, right here, right now.

Savor, she did. He kissed her, and she let him. She kissed him back, until she didn't know where she left off and he began. It was amazing. It was heady. It melted her from the inside out.

It might have gone on forever, had a sound from up above not penetrated her consciousness. She heard a little scrape of wood against wood. It almost sounded as if a window was being opened. She was still kissing Noah, her lips apart, their bodies in tune with a dance they hadn't experienced in more than a year.

The sound of wood scraping against wood came again. This time it was followed by a thud.

Noah must have heard it, too. His lips stopped moving against hers, and he held perfectly still.

The hollow thud of feet landing on the ground ten feet away severed the kiss in one fell swoop. She and Noah jerked apart and turned their heads. They saw the woman at the exact instant she saw them.

They all froze.

The young woman recovered first. She spun on her heel, dark brown hair nearly reaching her waist billowing like a curtain as she went.

"Wait!" Noah untangled his arms from Lacey's and started after her.

He saw her cut between the tavern and the store next door. He darted in after her, his breathing ragged, his eyes trained on the svelte creature pulling farther away. The space between the buildings was so narrow that his shoulders occasionally touched the bricks on either side as he ran. The walkway was lit only at the ends. Here in the center, he could barely make out the shape of the woman up ahead.

He was a fast runner. She was faster. Part gazelle, part acrobat, she scaled the wrought-iron gate that blocked the entry from Division Street, then bounded to the right without looking back. He went up the gate, too. From the top, he searched for a young woman with waist-length brown hair.

The Orchard Hill Theater had just let out, and throngs of people milled about the sidewalk. His gaze darted in every direction, but she seemed to have disappeared among them.

He jumped from the top of the gate. Landing lightly on his feet, he made a quick sweep up one side of Division Street and down the other. He didn't find her between buildings, in doorways or porticos. She might have literally disappeared.

It was no wonder Lacey called her Houdini. Like a siren or a forest sprite, she slipped out of buildings and scaled fences and seemed to disappear into thin air. The famous magician had used smoke and mirrors and a cape, and had taken the secret for his astonishing escapes with him to his grave. This girl's only cape was her long brown hair; her smoke and mirrors were her speed and agility. She had no assistant to wave her arms and draw the crowd's attention, no props or publicity. Her secret remained a mystery. And so did her identity.

Noah took a different route back to the alley, back to Lacey and to what was turning out to be a very unusual, though invigorating and interesting, second date.

Chapter Nine

When Noah returned to the alley, Lacey was sitting on the steps. She stood as he sauntered closer and, with a lift of her eyebrows, asked him a silent question. He answered just as silently with a shake of his head. Their mysterious Houdini remained at large.

The alley was losing its heat to the darkness and the stars their brightness to the blue haze of the mercury lights nearby. Many of the same people she'd noticed going toward Division Street earlier had already come by again in the opposite direction. As the murmur of voices grew distant, she and Noah returned to the place the young woman had been.

"I found something interesting," Lacey said, holding out her hand.

She showed him something that resembled a credit card. Taking it from her fingers, he held it to the light. "A bus pass?"

She nodded. "It's a prepaid bus pass. It must have fallen out of her pocket when she was climbing down."

"We don't know who she is," Noah said, handing the pass back to her. "We don't know where she came from, why she's here or where she's going, but apparently she's riding the city bus to get there."

Lacey peered up at the second-story window. "Now we also know how she's getting in and out of the tavern."

"What's up there?" Noah asked.

"Nothing much. The upstairs is a big empty

loft. My dad always talked about converting it into another apartment, but he never did."

"What's in the room directly below the window?" he persisted.

"The storage room. Why?"

Two stragglers wandered through the alley. Lacey and Noah took note of them out of habit as they passed. After a moment of quiet deliberation, he went to his truck and opened the passenger-side door. He rifled through the glove compartment, and returned with a slim flashlight. Sliding it into his back pocket, he said, "Did you get a good look at her?"

"I did."

"So did I. How old would you say she is?" he asked.

Lacey looked up at Noah's profile. He was studying the galvanized pipe that ran up the side of the building to the roof. It had been cut off six feet above the ground and capped years ago. It no longer served as a downspout, but the girl must have used it to climb up and down.

"She looked seventeen or eighteen to me. Not more than twenty," Lacey said.

"That's what I thought, too." A bead of perspiration trailed down the side of his face. His breathing was almost back to normal, though, his mind seemingly on the puzzle he was trying to solve. "She isn't Joey's mother." He said it so quietly he might have been thinking aloud.

Lacey felt her eyes widen. "Did you think she might have been?"

He was looking at her now. The moon and stars were competing with the mercury lights, but they were no competition for the glint in Noah's eyes as he nodded. "Her arrival coincided with Joey's, but the women Marsh and Reed are looking for are both over thirty. Something doesn't add up."

He wiped his hands on his jeans. Rubbing them together, he gave her a smile he reserved for situations involving risking life or limb or both, then reached high and grasped the pipe with both hands. He pulled himself up until he had a toehold, scaling the brick wall inches at a time. He gripped the pipe between his knees and ankles, reached out with one hand and carefully raised the window.

There was a victorious smile on his face when he looked down at Lacey. She gasped when he slipped, but he quickly regained his footing. It must have taken a great deal of concentration and agility to throw his left leg over the windowsill.

Before he could duck inside, she said, "You still think there's a connection, don't you, between the young woman we saw and Joey's mother?"

Balancing on the window ledge fifteen feet above the ground, he could have been an outlaw of old, his hair shaggy, his jaw darkened by a day-old beard, his golden-brown eyes delving into hers. "I believe in coincidence less and less every day," he said.

This wasn't the time or the place to discuss his philosophy regarding destiny, and yet she got the distinct impression he was including her in his statement. She had to admit that she felt energized by the idea that maybe it wasn't a co-incidence that she was back in Orchard Hill and Noah was back in Orchard Hill. Maybe there really was a method to the universe's madness.

"I'll meet you inside," he said.

"It's a date."

He looked down again and said, "I think it's time to proceed to step three." His voice was rich and sincere, but there was something lurking behind his grin, something unknown but not quite hidden.

On the brink of that precipice that was the rest of her life again, she ran up the newly painted stairs for her key.

Lacey had the back door open and the lights on inside the tavern when she heard footsteps overhead. The sound led her to the storage room where her father used to keep boxes of peanuts and pretzels, and crates of whiskey and scotch, and untapped kegs of beer. The shelves were crude and empty now, and all that remained was a leftover wooden crate and another whiskey barrel like the one she'd planted flowers in earlier.

A ceiling tile jiggled, and then it was being lifted away from above. The next thing she knew, Noah was lowering himself feetfirst through the opening.

He dropped lightly to the floor, brushed himself off and turned toward her. "It's hot up there. I'm not surprised she prefers it down here. She let herself downstairs through this ceiling tile, but she was using two windows to get in and out of the building, this one and one on the east side of the building. She may run like the wind but your Houdini left footprints that were easy to follow."

"Did she leave anything else?" Lacey asked.

"Nothing that I could find. Where's this bedroll she's been sleeping on?"

She led the way from the storeroom to the

back corner of the tavern. They both hunkered down at the far end of the pool table. The sleeping bag was still there but the snacks were gone.

"Tell me why you think she has something to do with Joey's arrival on your doorstep." She spoke quietly, reverently almost.

Resting his forearms on his thighs, Noah said, "It's just a hunch."

"What connection could she have to your situation?" she asked.

"I don't know, but the timing is right. As I said, it's just a hunch."

"You don't think she'll come back here again now, do you?" she asked.

"You know her better than I do. What do you think?"

They both stood up slowly.

A little taken aback by the fact that Noah seemed to understand Lacey's affinity for her guest, she said, "Whoever she is and whatever she's doing in Orchard Hill, she's street-smart. She won't want to risk getting caught. I almost wish we hadn't seen her. At least then she would be safe. Where will she sleep now?"

"You said it yourself," Noah replied. "She's street-smart. She'll find a safe place. If my hunch is right, and her arrival is somehow connected to Joey's, we haven't seen the last of her."

The idea chased Lacey's melancholy away. She couldn't explain it, but she felt a kinship with this unknown and mysterious young woman.

She shook out the sleeping bag. Folding it neatly, she left it on top of the pool table and added the bus pass, just in case the girl returned for either one.

Noah went to the storage room. Standing on an old crate, he slid the ceiling tile back into place. Lacey turned out the lights. They went out together, and she locked the door.

The wind had picked up, ruffling the collar of her airy shirt and sifting through his dark brown hair. He'd surprised her so many times today. It began when he'd offered to paint her steps, and continued when he'd asked to take that silly personality quiz, when he'd raced after her Houdini and when he'd climbed up the brick wall.

He surprised her again when he took her hand, and held, just held it. "I should go," he said. "Marsh and Reed are going to want to hear about our encounter with your Houdini. Madeline and Riley have invited all of us up to Traverse City for Sunday dinner tomorrow. I want to tell Marsh and Reed about tonight before they leave. I'm sure they're going to want to talk to Sam Lafferty."

"You're not going to Madeline's?" she asked.

"I have something more important to do tomorrow." His voice had taken on a sleepy huskiness that didn't necessarily mean he was sleepy again.

"More important than visiting your sister?" Lacey noticed her voice had grown a little husky, too.

He inched closer, his hand still cradling hers.

"After everything my baby sister has been through, believe me, she'll understand that what I'm planning for tomorrow needs to be my top priority."

"What are you planning for tomorrow?" she asked, her eyes on his.

"You don't really want me to spoil the surprise, do you?"

Her heart teetered slightly, because he was right. She wanted the anticipation, this prelude and, yes, she wanted to be surprised, even though waiting for surprises was almost unbearable.

"I *will* tell you this much," he said, his mouth a few inches from hers. "Tomorrow is the beginning of step three. I still have a lot to do, but I should be ready by five. Can I pick you up then?"

She nodded. And then he kissed her full on the mouth. He left her breathless and wanting, and eager to see him again.

* * *

The American flag Tom Bender raised to the top of the flagpole outside his office window every morning flapped in the breeze blowing across the tarmac. Lacey and Noah were caught between that same breeze and the warm air whirling from the propeller of Noah's newly restored Piper Cherokee.

He'd arrived to pick her up a few minutes early. His hair still damp from his shower, he'd wasted no time on small talk. "Are you ready?" he'd asked the moment she opened the door.

Ready? She'd taken a bubble bath, dried her hair, applied her makeup and changed her clothes four times. Oh, my, yes, was she ever ready. She was practically bursting with readiness.

"Where are we going?" she'd finally asked after he'd pulled onto Orchard Highway.

He crested a hill and said, "There's something I want to show you."

He was wearing blue jeans and a blue cotton

shirt with buttons down the front. When he turned into the county airfield, she was glad she'd decided on jeans, too. "Is your airplane finished?"

Noah didn't blame Lacey for being curious. Patience had never been her strong suit. Waiting until Christmas morning to open her presents had been excruciating for her. There was no hiding place she didn't discover, no wrapping paper she didn't tamper with. She was being a hell of a sport. A few minutes from now, he planned to make the wait worth her while.

When they'd first arrived at the airstrip, he'd gone inside to check the computer and radar. The wind had picked up an hour ago, and was coming straight out of the north, pressing a mass of hot air ahead of it. There was a thunderstorm sitting behind it, but the front was moving slowly. It was a little after six now and, as luck would have it, he was going to have plenty of time before it hit.

Just then his sleek white airplane taxied from

behind the first hangar. "My plane is finished," he said with a sense of undeniable pride, "but that's not the main attraction."

A Cessna landed on the second runway. Noah paid close attention to the engine speed and the sound of the brakes immediately after it touched down.

"Could you at least give me a hint?" she asked.

"I'd rather show you." He took her hand and led her out onto the tarmac where Digger was making another pass with Noah's plane. The Piper was a beauty, if he did say so himself. They'd finished her test run this morning, and she'd passed every inspection with flying colors. The engine hummed, the electrical system worked perfectly and so did the rudder, the propeller, the landing gear and ailerons, the beacon lights and navigational signal and every gauge on the dash. She'd been two years in the making and now she was all his.

"Is Digger going to fly the plane?" Lacey yelled. "Is that what you want to show me?"

Noah shook his head. For two years Digger had been helping Noah restore the Piper from a beat-up relic to this flight-ready beauty. All he would accept as payment was first taxiing rights after the last tweaking had been done. Noah could see Digger inside the cockpit, an old leather cap and goggles on his head and a big old smile on his face. Digger didn't fly—not anymore. One of these days he would deal with his issues, but not today.

He finished his loop around the airfield and brought her back to Noah. He cut the engine, opened the door and climbed down.

Lacey didn't know it yet, but Noah had faced the fear that had been eating at his insides since his parents' accident. As he took her fingers in his and led her to the plane, he'd never felt so free.

He ran his hand along the Piper's left wing. Next, he helped Lacey up. When he was in his seat, too, they fastened their belts. He flipped switches and started the engine. In almost no time they were rolling forward. He made adjustments for the direction and speed of the wind, and poured on the power.

He kept his eyes on the dials and instruments on the dash, his hands on the control wheel, his feet on the pedals on the floor. Ground lights and runway markers blurred in his peripheral vision. One second the plane was barreling across the ground. The next she was airborne.

Every takeoff was a thrill. This one was special. Not because he was flying his own airplane, although that added to the excitement, but because of the woman sitting in the noisy cockpit with him, her hair windblown, her cheeks pink, her eyes bluer than the sky.

He climbed to two thousand feet before he leveled off. He didn't see another airplane in the sky tonight, but in the distance was the Chestnut River. Two miles north of it was what Noah had been working on today.

He began his descent. When he was directly over his mark, he tipped the wing so Lacey could see all the way to the ground. He knew the moment she saw it, for her breath caught and her mouth opened.

Nine months out of the year, the meadow east of the orchard was just that, a meadow. Every autumn it became a parking lot for thousands of customers who visited Uncle Sully's Orchard to buy apples and pies, to ride in a horse-drawn wagon and attend craft shows and watch the cider press in action. This afternoon Noah had transformed it into something private.

Tears pooled in Lacey's eyes. She blinked them away, but more formed. She wasn't normally a crier, and didn't know what was wrong with her lately.

"Would you make another pass?" she asked. It wasn't easy for her to speak around the lump in her throat.

She didn't look at Noah. Instead, she kept her eyes trained on the terrain far below. She saw apple trees and rooftops and roads laid out in a grid pattern. He did as she requested. And then he was tipping the wing again, and there it was.

LACEY + NOAH was spelled out in white block letters. She stared at it until they flew past it again.

"How did you do that?"

"I wrote it with the same kind of chalk they use at the ballpark. I had to promise a free flight lesson next month in exchange for the use of their machine this afternoon, but that's a small price to pay. There's more." He climbed back to a safer altitude and said, "For years I flew away from you, Lacey Bell. Tonight, I'm coming back to you."

Her breath caught all over again. "Can you land down there?" she asked over the air leaks and engine noise.

"Do you want me to?" he asked.

She nodded.

She knew that Marsh kept the runway mowed for those occasions when Noah chose to land here. It was just a track through the old pasture, but it was long enough and it was a perfectly safe runway for small planes. Although he obviously hadn't planned to land here tonight, he radioed Tom and cleared it with him, as if he would grant her any wish at all.

"With this storm moving in, you'll have to wait until the wind changes to take off again," Tom warned.

"I'll park her on low ground," Noah said into the radio. "Don't wait up."

Lacey's gaze met his.

"Ten-four, pal, and give Lacey a kiss for me."

He set the plane down lightly. Landings were always loud. Because of the grassy track, this one was bumpy, too. He brought the Piper to a complete stop with plenty of runway to spare. Directly ahead of them was Lacey's name in big white letters.

"I can't believe you went to all this trouble," she said.

"A woman like you deserves a grand gesture. I thought about having a banner made and flying it behind my plane, but you're too private for that. This is intimate, for you alone."

Lacey had always known Noah had a noble streak and a heart of gold. She'd had no idea he was sentimental, too.

"Come on," she said, removing her seat belt. "I want to see it up close."

Noah got out first. Reaching up for her, his hands went to her waist, lingering even after her feet touched the ground. The branches in the nearby cottonwoods sang in the evening breeze. There was something romantic about the sound of the wind. Romance, it seemed, was everywhere.

"If I forget to tell you later," she said, "I had fun tonight."

He leaned down. For a moment she thought he intended to kiss her on the mouth. He surprised her once again when his lips brushed her cheek instead. Holding perfectly still, she closed her eyes, for there was something incredibly touching about the whisper of a man's lips on a woman's cheek. It was a first for her.

"Believe me, I'm planning to make tonight so memorable you'll never forget it."

It was so like him that she couldn't help laughing out loud. Noah Sullivan might have been on his best behavior, but he was no choirboy.

Thank heavens.

"You sound awfully sure of yourself, flyboy." She darted away, toward the letters in his name.

Noah let Lacey go, but he didn't let her out of his sight. He knew what she wanted. It so happened that he wanted the same thing. What an understatement. Before the night was through, they were going to make love. He'd been planning for it all day.

He'd written his message to her on the downward slope of a grassy hill. He'd flown over it twice, driving back and forth in order to tweak it to get the lettering just right. Now Lacey was walking along the lower edge of his message. Unable to contain her joy, she did a cartwheel and laughed out loud. Her arms outstretched, her hair streaming behind her like an aviator's scarf, she wove in and out of the letters in his message. The woman held nothing back. She never had. His body heated the way it had the first time they'd made love.

At eighteen she'd been a lot like him, a little beaten up by life, slightly belligerent and very bold. The guys around the pool hall used to say she was easy. She'd been an enchantress who knew her own mind, what she liked and whom she'd wanted. For some unexplainable reason, she'd wanted him. Back then he'd been so full of himself that he'd seen no reason to deny her. If he could go back and do one thing differently, he would change the way he'd taken her that first time. But he hadn't known. Like everyone else, he'd assumed she'd been experienced.

He'd been wrong, for there had been blood on her sheets, and afterward, he'd heard her crying in the bathroom. Uncertain about what to do, he'd gone in to talk to her, and wound up wrapping his arms around her. He would have been content to do just that, but she'd had other ideas. Lacey Bell wasn't one to stay down for the count.

In the past two-and-a-half years they'd been intimate on only one occasion, and that had been more than a year ago. When she'd first broken it off, he'd tried to eradicate her memory every chance he had. He couldn't remember a single face, and yet he'd never forgotten hers. He hadn't admitted it out loud, but he hadn't been with anybody since that night a year ago after her father's funeral.

"What's next?" she called.

She stood near the bottom of the hill, her hair blowing in the wind, her jeans low and her black knit shirt just tight enough to be interesting. He walked closer, his stride long and purposeful. "What I'd planned to do was have a picnic. And then I was going to seduce you."

Her chest heaved with the deep breath she took. "That sounded like past tense to me."

He heard himself chuckle. "That's because I didn't plan to land here. The grinders and drinks are in a cooler in my truck at the airfield."

He was only four feet away when she said, "As luck would have it, I had a late lunch."

His body heated a little more.

"Do you think you could kiss me now?" she asked.

"I don't think anything could keep me from kissing you."

They came together on a rush of air and joy. The kiss was an explosion of heat and need and everything earthy. His hands were in her hair, on her back, at her waist, but his mouth never left hers. Her curves molded to the contours of his hard body, and desire unlike anything he'd ever felt kicked through him at three g's.

His arms tightened around her as they dropped to their knees on the soft grass, the wind whipping her hair into both their faces. The low-hanging clouds formed an arc over their little haven, making the meadow feel secluded and exotic. They remained on their knees, their bodies tight together, their mouths connected the way solder joined metal.

The sprinkles came first. Warm and gentle, they fell from the low clouds, soaking into their clothes and dampening their hair. Too soon the sprinkles turned to rain. Then the thunder came. It rolled and rumbled, shaking the ground until they both felt its vibration in their knees.

Noah cast a look to the sky as lightning forked in the west. "It's going to get dangerous to be out here," he said, drawing her to her feet. "We'd better make a run for the house."

She looked up at the clouds and then at the rain falling to the meadow. "It's going to wash away your note."

"Only from the grass," he said. "Never from here." He pressed a fist to his chest.

"What about your airplane?"

"They're not predicting strong winds. The Piper's on low ground. She'll be fine."

They started toward the house at a jog,

building to a steady run. They followed the lane through the west orchard, emerging into the clearing at the foot of the hill leading to the house, winded. It was pouring by the time they reached the back door. Although it was only seven o'clock, it seemed like much later.

The clock on the stove ticked and the rain pattered against the window. Otherwise, the big old house was quiet and empty.

Noah brought them each a towel from the bathroom downstairs. "We have the house to ourselves," he said as the lights flickered off, then on again.

"How long?" she asked, drying her face and hair.

"For a few more hours, at least."

Invigorated by the run and the landing and the storm, he dropped their towels to the back of a kitchen chair and reached for both her hands. He drew her to him and kissed her again, long and slow and deep.

The next time lightning struck, the lights went

out and stayed out. It was too early to need candles or a flashlight, so, without saying a word, he led the way up the back staircase.

Partway up the stairs Lacey thought about the scars on her abdomen. Other than her doctor, no man had seen them. Noah would be the first. She would tell him how she'd gotten them, and what they meant for her future. It would be a relief to finally tell someone, especially someone who'd gone to so much trouble to tell her how he felt about her.

The back hallway was narrow, the floors old and creaky. It was their music. The rain on the roof was their refrain, and Noah's murmurs and Lacey's sighs as his arms came around her in his room was the most amazing melody.

Not much had changed since she'd been here last. His bed was on the wall opposite the window where it had always been. There was a lamp and an alarm clock and a dresser and a bedside table, too. Outside, lightning zigzagged out of the low black clouds.

Noah quickly closed the window and drew the blinds. While nature put on a light show between the slats in the blinds, he placed his hands on her shoulders.

How many times had she seen him looking at her this way? How many times had she looked back at him, her eyes wide in the semidarkness, her thoughts gentle as she tried to commit the sight of him to memory?

She stepped closer to her bad boy turned knight in shining armor and unfastened his first button. Beneath his damp shirt, she felt his heart rate quicken. She could tell by the slow deep breath he took that he was trying to be patient and let her take her time. His patience lasted until she loosened the second button.

And then he took over. He undid them all and peeled the wet garment off, turning it inside out in the process. Her black shirt was next. His eyes were on her now. She thrilled at the way his gaze heated as she reached behind her and unfastened her bra.

He had her in his arms, a hand on her breast, his eyes closed deliriously. Moaning softly, she closed her eyes, too. Belt buckles jangled and zippers were lowered and jeans came off. Wearing only a wisp of black lace, she shivered, but she was only chilled on the surface. Everywhere else there was only heat.

He whipped the summer quilt off his bed and held the sheet for her. She climbed in, and he followed her. Between the smooth layers of thin cotton, their legs entwined.

She lay on her side now, and he lay on his. He touched the tip of her chin with the outer edge of his hand, slowly trailing to the little hollow at the base of her neck, down the center of her chest, grazing her breasts, each in turn, with the back of his hand.

He found her mouth with his lips, working magic there. And then he moved his magic elsewhere. He began at that sensitive little spot below her ear, moved to the ticklish hollow on her shoulder and, finally, to her breasts. She wound her fingers through his rain-dampened hair, along his ears, to his shoulders and the corded muscles of his back. As thunder rumbled, they rolled across the bed, lips trailing, hearts quickening, breaths rasping and deepening in turns.

She didn't tell him how wonderful it felt to be back in his arms. Instead, she showed him with every kiss, every sigh, every touch and murmur and groan and lusty cry for more.

"You're wild," he told her.

But she wasn't the only wild person in this bed. In some far corner of her mind, she was aware that he'd leaned over the side of the bed and was rifling through a drawer. He came back to her with a small foil package between his teeth.

He tore it open, and said, "I hope these things don't have an expiration date."

She didn't understand what he meant.

Until he said, "Hopefully they're good for longer than a year."

For a moment she thought she'd heard wrong. Noah had gone an entire year without making love? Her heart rose up to her throat again. She took him in her hand and said, "You don't need to use anything. I won't get pregnant."

"You're sure?"

She nodded. She thought he might question this further. Obviously he trusted her. She knew they would have to talk about this, and soon.

He tossed the packet over his shoulder, and came to her, thigh to thigh, belly to belly, breast to chest, his lips on hers. And the time for talking and for coherent thought came to an end.

She lost track of who touched whom, of who was on top, and of where he left off and she began as he took her breast in his big hand, and slowly, reverently almost, lowered his mouth to her soft flesh. His other hand wandered to her belly, and slipped beneath the lace edge of her panties. After he'd drawn them down her legs and slowly eased on top of her, and brought his mouth to hers, she only knew that whatever happened from this moment on really was the beginning of something brand-new.

Chapter Ten

Noah was sprawled on his back, his pillow mysteriously missing from the bed, a corner of the sheet all that covered him. His head rested on one arm while the other arm dangled off the side of the bed, his fingers grazing the floor. Beside him, Lacey lay on her stomach, her face turned toward him.

Night had fallen and the storm had moved on, leaving behind only a steady rain. The power must have come back on. He could feel the cool air blasting from the vent, but he hadn't turned on a lamp in here. In the black-pearl darkness, he could barely tell that Lacey's eyes were closed.

"I might never move again," he said. He was that relaxed, that spent, that satisfied. Especially that.

She made a sound deep in her throat that meant ditto.

It was no wonder they were both practically comatose, though. Three hours of sex did that to a person. Make that three hours of Lacey.

Soft and supple where he was hard and solid, she was thinner than he remembered, but wilder and lustier, and somehow freer with her passion. The first time they'd made love tonight, he'd taken his time, drawing every last sigh out of her until she'd cried out for release.

The next time she'd set the pace, and what a pace it was. When the sheets got tangled, they'd kicked them off. Thunder had rumbled and lightning had flickered, but the storm was nothing compared to the crescendo they created with every kiss and touch and sigh and moan. He'd used his hands and his mouth and every inch of his body to show her how he felt, and she'd shown him her feelings in countless ways, too.

All day he'd planned to seduce her, but even he couldn't have planned that last time. He'd been feeling pretty damn satisfied as he'd gathered up their damp shirts and jeans and carried them down to the dryer in the basement. He hadn't bothered getting dressed, and she hadn't heard him pad back up the stairs barefoot. He'd found her on her knees on the floor, looking under the bed for her other sandal. Even in the semidarkness, one glimpse of that delectable backside of hers was all it had taken. He'd had to have her again. When it was over they were both seeing stars.

Step three was off to a great start. Spent and sated and half-asleep now, he really might never move again.

"I'm starving," she said sleepily.

He made a grizzly bear sort of reply.

"Are you?" she asked.

"Now that you mention it. What are you hungry for?"

"A cheeseburger and fries and a hot-fudge sundae."

He chuckled because she'd obviously given it some thought. She'd always had a hearty appetite. Although half the time he didn't know where she put it, he liked that about her. In fact, he couldn't think of anything he didn't like about her.

Resigning himself to the fact that he had to move sooner or later anyway, he swung his feet off the bed. "Your clothes are probably dry by now."

"What time is it?" She sat up, too.

"A little before ten."

She caught him looking at her breasts from the light spilling from the hallway. Pointing to the door, she said, "Food, I need food. And The Hill closes at eleven on Sundays."

He scooped up the foil packet he'd opened but hadn't used, and tossed it in the wastebasket on his way out the door. She'd assured him that he didn't need it. Women knew their cycles, but the truth was he wouldn't have minded if he'd gotten her pregnant tonight. It had been surprising enough when he'd experienced those brief twinges that night when Joey first arrived. He'd almost been disappointed Joey wasn't his son. This was a complete change of heart. He wondered what Lacey would say if she knew. It wasn't something he could just blurt out. So instead, he said, "I'll be right back with your clothes."

Lacey waited until Noah left the room to make a run for the bathroom. As she was closing the door, she saw that he was walking away from her toward the top of the stairs.

Lacey knew that confident swagger, that attitude. She was tempted to call him back to her all over again. Hungry or not, she would have enjoyed making love again. But Noah went downstairs and she closed the bathroom door and began to freshen up. After all, they didn't have to make up for lost time or try to fit a week's worth of memories into one night. They were starting anew, and this was just the beginning.

She'd never felt so full of hope and enthusiasm for tomorrow and the day after that. The future really was wide-open.

Like so many big, rambling old houses, the upstairs bathroom had been installed long after the house had been built. Once a closet, it contained a narrow shower, a toilet and an old-fashioned pedestal sink. There was a mirrored medicine cabinet over the sink and another mirror on the back of the door.

She stood at the sink, looking at her reflection. Her hair was a mess. Since there was no saving her smudged mascara, she scrubbed her face clean. She found a hairbrush in an old cabinet and an old tube of Madeline's lip gloss and mascara. After applying a little of both, she glanced over her shoulder at the mirror on the door. She started to turn away. Only to stop.

For the past six months, she'd stayed away from full-length mirrors, preferring not to dwell on what was below her waist. Tonight, she took a long look at her entire reflection. What she saw was a twenty-eight-year-old woman with dark hair and blue eyes, pouty lips and full breasts. There was a whisker burn on her neck and a heart-shaped birthmark above her waist. Two scars crisscrossed her belly below it. The lines had faded from red to pink in the past six months. A year from now they would lighten to the color of her skin.

She'd forgotten about them while she and Noah had been making love. That second time she would have been hard-pressed to remember her name if asked. As it turned out, it had been too dark to see them, after all. When the time was right she would tell Noah about her ruptured appendix and the internal scarring that had resulted from the subsequent infection.

She would tell him that the likelihood that she would conceive a child was somewhere between slim and none. She wasn't pretending that she wasn't still sad about it. There might always be a sensitive little spot where that wish for a baby of her own had been, but her incisions weren't the only things that were fading. Hope and happiness were magnificent healers. Still, she couldn't help reflecting on the irony of it all, for the reason she'd broken things off with Noah two-and-a-half years ago was because she'd wanted children and he didn't. Fate had stepped in. Now a future with or without children was no longer an issue between her and Noah.

Placing a hand on her belly, she waited for the anguish and searing disappointment. Perhaps it was the lingering effects of euphoria following all that amazing sex, but she felt the first stirring of acceptance.

She donned her bra and panties. Hearing him moving around his bedroom, she peeked out and discovered her dry clothes right outside the bathroom door. Her shirt and jeans were slightly warm from the dryer. Still wearing that beatific smile, she left the washroom. Noah had called tonight step three.

Step three had only just begun.

The founding fathers of Orchard Hill had been a pragmatic group of loosely connected men whose families had originally emigrated from Scotland. It was said that they'd wasted nothing. Even middle names were an extravagance to them, and were rarely bestowed. It wasn't surprising that the town had been laid out just as pragmatically, the streets named for numbers and trees and a president or two. It stood to reason that they'd called the path through the very center of the grid Division Street. Intersecting streets fell away to the Chestnut River in the west and to the orchards in the east. It was only fitting that businesses lined either side of the wide avenue. Also fitting was the name of the town's oldest restaurant, which happened to sit on the highest elevation in town.

After all these years, people didn't frequent The Hill because it was aptly named. They came here because the food was always good and the gossip even better.

Decorated in early Americana diner style, the restaurant had been surprisingly crowded when Lacey and Noah arrived at a little after ten. Now, fifteen minutes before closing time, only a handful of customers remained. That didn't detract from the hometown ambiance. It did, however, make the sound of the trio whooping it up in a booth near the back audible in every corner of the room.

Lacey didn't remember the last time she'd laughed so much, or loved so much, or eaten so much, for that matter, and all in the same day. She and Noah had been tucking away the last of their burgers and fries with loads of ketchup when a large man with a shaved head stopped at their table.

Noah was completely nonplussed by the man's unexpected appearance. Ever since he'd climbed out of bed that last time, he'd been so cool, calm and collected that she doubted anything could ruffle his feathers. She was a little surprised when he introduced the man as Sam Lafferty, the P.I. Marsh and Reed had hired, but she wasn't surprised that he and Noah were friends.

Noah had friends everywhere.

Lacey liked the private investigator almost immediately. He'd told Noah about a call he'd gotten from Marsh regarding some woman named Houdini. Lacey and Noah had told him what they'd discovered. Before he followed a lead on a waitress in Texas, he wanted to get as detailed a description as possible. He was going to pay the Sullivans a visit. Marsh and Reed were due home in an hour, and Sam had decided to kill a little time at The Hill.

The P.I. was a giant and might have seemed intimidating, with his muscular arms, shaved head and pierced ear, but he'd been genuinely pleased to be invited to sit with them. He was either a fast healer or tough as nails, because she didn't see any evidence of the boot he'd taken in his face a few days ago.

From what she could gather, the life of a P.I. was solitary and messy. Sam sure wasn't lacking in entertaining stories. Most of them began with the same three words.

"There I was, minding my own business, and in walked an old mark who was supposed to be in jail."

Or "There I was with a doughnut in one hand and a pair of binoculars in the other."

Or "There I was, staring down the wrong end of a Smith & Wesson."

She didn't know how he'd had time to finish his hot-fudge sundae with all the talking he'd done. If half of what he said was true, he was lucky to be alive.

Noah's sundae was gone now, too. Free, his right hand found its way beneath the table to her knee. He squeezed her leg gently, and moved up a few inches. Heat bloomed in places not directly connected to her knee.

She kept her eyes on her parfait glass, anticipation melting her insides as if she were made of ice cream, too. On the other side of the booth, Sam launched into another tale.

"There I was," he said in his booming voice, "handcuffed to a headboard in my birthday suit, when in walked my date's old flame. It was a real mood breaker, let me tell you. A jealous ex-lover is more dangerous than a roomful of rattlesnakes."

"How did you manage to get out of that one?" Lacey couldn't help asking.

"Sometime I'll have to show you the trophy headboard—" Sam began.

"Hanging on his wall," Noah said.

They'd spoken in unison, and shook their heads the same way. Looking from one to the other, it occurred to Lacey that this was a side of Noah she didn't know anything about.

"How did you two meet?" she asked.

Her question launched another "There I was" story that had Lacey laughing all over again. It didn't bother her that Sam Lafferty was one part bluster and the rest Irish bull. She liked him.

She liked men, even the dangerous ones. She would be forever grateful to the women who'd taught her about the facts of life and how to hold her head high and how a knee placed just so could render a man defenseless, but it was one very special man who'd taught her compassion.

It was a well-known fact that her mom had been gone by the time Harlan Bell bought a rundown bar on Division Street. A lot of people thought her father had been too lenient with Lacey when she was growing up. She'd even overheard a few say he had no business raising a daughter when he spent most of his time pouring drinks for deadbeats and losers downstairs. But those people—her well-meaning teachers, mostly—hadn't seen the way her father had taken care of his family before they'd moved from Ohio to Orchard Hill.

They could think what they wanted, but they hadn't awakened in the middle of the night to the croon of her dad's deep voice in the next room when her mom was in too much pain to sleep. Night after night, day after day, through doctor visits and disappointments, he'd held Lacey and her mom up, and he'd gotten them all through it. So, yes, Lacey liked men, especially men like her father, a-little-rough-around-the-edges types with bawdy stories and honorable souls. If she had to venture a guess, she would say that Sam Lafferty was one of those.

The P.I. dropped a five spot on the table and slid from the booth. "Want me to tell Marsh and Reed not to wait up?"

"That's not the kind of thing you say in front of a lady, Sam," Noah answered.

"I don't doubt that Lacey is a hell of a lady. I'm just saying it's been ten minutes since I've seen your hand."

Once again, Lacey laughed out loud. Sam Lafferty hadn't earned the reputation as one of the best P.I.s in the state by being unobservant. When Noah lifted his hand, Lacey's came up with it, her fingers laced with his.

"You've been holding her hand? You've got it bad, pal." Shaking his head, Sam ambled out of the restaurant. Lacey and Noah sauntered to the front counter to pay for their meals.

"How was everything?" the tired waitress asked.

"Wonderful," Lacey replied. "Everything is wonderful."

The other woman put the money Noah handed her in the drawer and counted out his change. "Yes," she said, "I can see that."

Rosy Sirrine was tall and had sturdy hips and steady hands. As much a fixture in Orchard Hill as the sculpture on the town square, her ethnicity was a mystery. Nobody could remember a time when she hadn't been head waitress here, yet there was no gray in her black braid.

She reminded Lacey of an old nursery rhyme about a wise old owl. The more she saw, the less she spoke, the less she spoke, the more she heard, or something to that effect. "What are you doing working the late shift?" Lacey asked.

"Dora went down to the courthouse today and got married. She up and quit without any notice," Rosy said drolly. "I was planning to call you tomorrow. Are you still looking for a job?"

Lacey was aware of Noah beside her, but she kept her eyes on Rosy. "I've picked up a temporary position, but I don't know how long it'll last. What hours would you need me?"

"What hours could you give me?"

"I have a temporary job, but I could work evenings for now."

"That would be a great help," Rosy said.

Try as she might, Lacey couldn't help asking, "Who did Dora marry?"

Dora Peterson had worked here almost as long as Rosy. She had her hair washed, curled, coifed and shellacked every week at the Do-Da Salon around the corner, and batted her fake eyelashes at every man who walked through the door.

"Henry finally found somebody to accept his proposal," Rosy replied.

"Henry Brewbaker?" Noah quipped.

Lacey remembered when the old sweetheart had proposed to her.

"It was only a matter of time before somebody saw the opportunity and took it." Rosy pressed her lips together as if she'd put a tick-a-lock on them.

"Are you upset that you've lost your best waitress?" Lacey asked.

Rosy made a sound through her pursed lips.

And Noah said, "Rosy would never stand in the way of true love, Lace. It's a pity, though, if she's lost her best customer."

Rosy smiled, proving that not even she was immune to Noah's charm. After a little more discussion regarding her hours, it was decided that Lacey would hold both jobs for the time being, thereby giving Marsh and Reed time to hire a replacement and perhaps a permanent nanny. She would begin here tomorrow night at six.

Noah took Lacey's hand again as they left the restaurant. He held her door, then walked around to the driver's side of Reed's Mustang, which he'd borrowed for the occasion because his truck was still at the airfield.

It would have been just as fast to walk to her apartment, but she enjoyed the short drive. It was as if every one of her senses was heightened. The radio hummed and the car purred and the late-night air felt blessedly cool after the rain. It was all somehow sweeter because of the man at her side.

Noah walked her to her door, but he waited to kiss her until they were both inside. All of a sudden she was in his arms again, and he was kissing her as if it had been months since he'd worked his magic on her lips.

She was coming to expect that every kiss would sweep her off her feet. This one didn't disappoint. Wet, wild and possessive, it left her breathless and opening her mouth for more.

Her head tipped back, need uncurling all over again. She glided her hands around his waist, catching in the folds of his cotton shirt along the way. He pressed his body to hers, seeking what she was seeking. And then, with Herculean strength of will, he tore his mouth from hers.

Resting his forehead against hers, he said, "Damn. Reed, Marsh and Sam are expecting me. Leaving you like this is getting old."

She brought one hand to his cheek. "Your brothers are lucky to have you. You should be proud of yourself for everything you're doing for them."

His brown eyes widened. She was pretty sure a slap wouldn't have surprised him more. He seemed uncomfortable with her praise. Finally, he said, "It was a lot easier being the hell-raising, no-good brother."

"You were never no-good, but this feels good, doesn't it?" she asked.

A certain look entered his eyes. "Are we still talking about pride?"

She pushed playfully at his shoulders. "You have a dirty mind."

But she noticed that he was smiling. She stepped away from the door so he could open it. "I'll see you in the morning, Lace."

From the doorway she watched him drive away in his brother's Mustang. "I'll see you in the morning," she whispered into the vast night sky.

She closed the door, eventually, and wandered through the small apartment, pinching herself. It was hard to believe that only a week ago she'd stood in the smelly exhaust fumes of a Greyhound bus, three suitcases and her camera all she had to her name. It had seemed there was little hope of happiness for the future.

Now she was driving a borrowed car and living in an uncluttered apartment that smelled like the rain-freshened air wafting through the window tonight. She had friends who cared about her, and little ones who called her Aunt Lacey.

She'd lived in Chicago for more than two years, but this felt like home. She had roots here, and now she had two jobs instead of none.

Her life had purpose here. April had shown someone else through the tavern. One of these days, it would sell, and she would pay off her debt to the hospital in Chicago.

And she had the feeling that the best part of her new life was yet to come.

Chapter Eleven

Marsh, Reed and Joey were at the kitchen table when Lacey arrived for work Monday morning. Marsh smiled absently at her after she let herself in. Moving Joey to his shoulder, he turned his attention back to Reed and whatever they were doing on his laptop.

The coffeemaker stopped gurgling while she was washing her hands at the kitchen sink. Wondering where Noah was, she poured the steaming liquid into two mugs and carried them to the table. Again, Marsh smiled absently at her.

Reed said a quick thank-you and continued typing.

She turned back to Marsh and held out her hands for Joey. "When was his last bottle?" she asked quietly.

"A little after six o'clock. He slept through the night," Marsh said.

"We never heard a peep out of him," Reed added without looking up from his screen.

"We don't know what came over him. Noah, either, for that matter."

"Noah isn't awake yet?" she asked.

"Last I knew he was still sleeping like a baby," Marsh answered.

Smiling warmly at Joey, she walked around the room with him, rocking him in her arms. Today she was going to give him a bath and then at least twenty minutes of tummy time to strengthen his back and arms. She was going to read to him, too. According to her library book, it was never too early to begin.

Gazing up at her, he studied her face so

intently he didn't even blink. He was a very serious baby. She'd noticed that when he smiled, he put his heart into it. Already his eyelashes were long and dark. It was too soon to tell if his eyes would stay blue, like Reed's, or turn brown, like Marsh's.

She looked at Marsh and Reed, searching their faces for similarities to Joey. Focusing on whatever they were doing on Reed's computer, they were both clean-shaven, their hair, although different colors, clipped short. They had similar noses and builds. They would never be able to determine which of them was Joey's father through appearance alone. She didn't think it was her place to bring up the DNA test.

"How does this sound?" Reed took another sip of his hot coffee. Resting his elbows on the table, he said, "Wanted—Professional nanny for three-month-old baby boy. Weekdays from nine to five. Degree in early childhood development preferred."

"Experience required," Marsh said, lifting his mug to his mouth.

Evidently, they were composing an ad for a nanny.

"And references—don't forget those," Marsh added.

Reed typed another line then asked, "What about transportation?"

Joey grinned up at Lacey. It was as if he knew all this was for him.

"Preferably something with a good crash rating," Marsh said.

"She can't be too young," Reed said.

"Just say she should wear her hair in a bun and must smell like fresh-baked bread." Lacey, Marsh and Reed all turned as Noah sauntered into the room. Looking as if he'd just rolled out of bed, he wore his usual faded jeans and a gray T-shirt with fold marks down the center. His hair was mussed and his feet were bare.

"Very funny," Marsh said.

Noah ignored him. He hadn't taken his eyes

off Lacey. She wasn't sure what he was up to, but she held still as he took Joey from her. Admittedly, it was most likely an accident when the back of his hand brushed her breast in the process. It was no accident that he noticed.

He carried Joey across the room, his fingertips meeting at the baby's sturdy back. "You can have her back in a minute, buddy," he said to the baby, "but you have to share."

Handing Joey to Marsh, he sauntered back to Lacey and kissed her on the mouth right there in the kitchen in front of God and everyone. Brief but powerful, it was a firm kiss, a possessive kiss, an I've-missed-you-and-it's-only-been-ten-hours kiss. When it was over, he gave her a cocky grin and strolled back for Joey.

Lacey saw the look Reed and Marsh exchanged. *Ah,* it said. *So that's why Noah slept like a baby.*

She was too familiar with them to mind. How could she mind, when they'd taken the news that they needed to find another nanny in stride the way they took everything in stride?

When Joey was back in Lacey's arms, Noah poured himself a cup of coffee then joined his brothers at the table. Their personalities were as different as their choices in clothing. And yet there was no denying the family resemblance. Every one of them exuded enough pheromones to be dangerous. As she carried Joey from the room to prepare for his bath, she doubted that even grandmother types would be immune.

Noah was whistling when he pushed through the back door. Letting the screen bang shut behind him, he slung his duffel bag over his shoulder and descended the porch steps. His gait was loose, his stride long and sure. He'd just kissed Lacey goodbye, and although he'd thrown a change of clothes in his duffel, he was hoping he wouldn't be gone all night. He wanted to come back and do that again as soon as possible.

For now, he was on his way to the meadow and his airplane. He cut across the side lawn where the old wooden swing swayed slightly in the gentle breeze, and started down the lane. Sam was meeting him at the airfield. From there they were flying to Dallas and what Sam hoped was a lead on the woman from Reed's past.

Noah was halfway to the meadow when he saw the ATV parked near the cider house up ahead. Not far from the four-wheel-drive utility vehicle was a pile of mangled ivy. He didn't see Marsh, though.

His brother had a vendetta against the invasive vine. Nobody knew who'd planted the damn nuisance, but generations of Sullivan men had been battling it ever since. Sometimes it disappeared for a year or two, only to sneak back up the stone exterior of the cider house when nobody was looking. It had become a test of wills, and so far Marsh and the ivy were neck and neck.

"How about a ride to your airplane?"

Noah turned around at the sound of Marsh's voice, and found his brother just off the beaten path under one of the trees he'd grafted years ago.

"I'd take a ride to my plane," Noah said.

There was something about the way Marsh strode toward him that gave Noah the impression that his brother had been waiting for him. He had no idea what was going on in his older brother's mind. Marsh was a tough nut to crack. They were alike that way.

Marsh hopped on the ATV and Noah flung a leg over the seat behind him. Within minutes, they arrived at the meadow where Noah had parked his airplane last night.

They scattered a flock of sparrows and elicited a scolding from a pair of crows. It was another warm June morning with blue skies and sunshine. The ground had softened and the grass had greened and dandelions were blooming like a thousand little suns.

As Noah climbed off the quad, he noticed

that the chalk had been washed away. "Thanks, Marsh. Sam and I will let you and Reed know as soon as we find this waitress named Cookie." Duffel bag in hand, he started toward his airplane.

"Hey, Noah, have you got a minute?"

Noah turned around, his gaze taking in his brother from head to toe. Neither of them wore sunglasses and both were squinting. They were dressed similarly, too, but moisture had wicked up the hem of Marsh's jeans.

The morning was quiet now that the quad wasn't running and the birds had disappeared. Marsh was quiet, too. That was nothing new. Reed was the talker in the family.

"Whatcha need?" Noah asked.

"You've been flying us all over kingdom come for the better part of a week." Marsh slid his hand into his front pocket.

"You know me. I was born to fly. Besides, it feels good to pay you back."

Marsh wore a look of genuine surprise. "Pay me back for what?"

"Oh, this and that." Noah couldn't quite pull off a nonchalant shrug.

Marsh folded his arms, a sign that he wasn't going anywhere until Noah came clean. His oldest brother was like the damn ivy, tenacious and determined. "Pay me back for what?" he repeated.

"For giving up your future for me and Madeline when Mom and Dad died, for one thing."

Suddenly Marsh was only an arm's length away. "Why would you think I gave up my future for you?"

"Because you did."

"The hell I did. You remind me so much of Dad sometimes I can't believe it."

This was news to Noah. Marsh's genuine surprise convinced Noah that this wasn't the reason he'd put himself in Noah's path this morning.

"As long as we're on the subject, thank you. If you and Reed hadn't stepped in, Madeline and I probably would have wound up living with the judge."

Marsh grinned, just as Noah had hoped he would. "There were times I considered threatening you with that, but for your information, I didn't give up anything. Coming back to the orchard was what I'd always wanted to do. Keeping our family together was an honor and a privilege."

"All the hell I put you through was a privilege? Are you crazy?"

"All this guilt you've been carrying around has been for nothing," Marsh said. "Who's the crazy one?"

They wore similar smug expressions.

"I want to talk to you about something else," Marsh said.

"Make it quick. I've gotta pick Sam up and gas the plane at the airfield."

"You and Lacey looked pretty happy this morning."

Noah thought about the expression on Lacey's

face when he'd told her goodbye a few minutes ago. Her hands full of slippery baby, she'd smiled at him through the sprinkles Joey was sending up as he kicked his feet and flailed his arms, and Noah hadn't wanted to leave.

"As soon as I get up the nerve," he said, "I'm going to ask her to marry me."

"No kidding? Good for you. That's what I wanted to talk to you about."

Marsh reached into his pocket for something. He extended his hand toward Noah and slowly opened his fingers.

Noah stared at the treasure in his brother's palm. Emotion thickened his voice as he said, "That was Mom's. Reed and I think you should have it."

All around Noah the sun-kissed meadow came to life. Birds sang and insects buzzed and the breeze combed through his hair like a mother's hand. He had to clear his throat in order to speak. "What about Madeline?" he asked.

"It was her idea."

A lump lodged in Noah's throat.

As if he knew the moment called for drastic measures, Marsh shoved his hand closer and said, "Take it already. You have a plane to fuel and I have ivy to eradicate."

Wrapping his fingers around the delicate heirloom, Noah didn't know what to say, except, "I can't believe you thought about dumping me at the judge's."

Marsh took his time smiling, and the rite of passage was complete. He climbed on the quad and Noah climbed into the cabin of his airplane. From the cockpit he watched Marsh speed back to his orchard. The lump in his throat dissolved and his heart beat a steady rhythm.

He checked gauges and radioed the airfield. The minute he was cleared for takeoff, he raced down the grass runway. As he lifted off, he'd never been more proud to be a Sullivan.

By the end of the day they should know more about the identity of this woman named Cookie. As soon as he could, he would be flying home again. And when he did, he was going to make Lacey an offer he hoped to high heaven she couldn't refuse.

All these years Noah had been convinced that Marsh was the family man who'd given up his future for Noah and Madeline. He'd somehow believed that Reed had given up an urban lifestyle for the same reason. Now Noah realized they were all family men at heart. Wasn't Lacey going to be surprised?

The first thing Lacey did after she let herself into her apartment at nine-thirty that night was open every window. When she'd stopped home earlier to change her clothes before going to The Hill, she'd peeked inside the tavern. The sleeping bag and bus pass lay undisturbed on the pool table where she'd left them.

The second thing she did after getting home was peel off her clothes and turn on the shower. Lathering her hair and washing the day's grime down the drain helped, but the effects didn't last long in the hot, airless apartment.

The third thing she did was admit that the stuffy apartment and the fact that her Houdini hadn't returned weren't the reasons she felt so listless. She couldn't even blame her aching feet and the dull headache she'd brought home with her after her first shift serving up food to the supper crowd at The Hill.

Noah was still in Texas.

She'd known there was a possibility he wouldn't make it back until tomorrow. She'd just seen him twelve hours before. There was no reason for her to feel so out of sorts.

She padded to the living room and yawned. Holding two jobs was tiring. She should just go to bed.

She aimed the remote at the television, adjusted the rabbit ears, aimed the remote at the little black digital-converter box again and repeated the process. Even with the ball of aluminum foil on the top of each ear, only three stations came in. One was a police drama, two were reality shows and all were slightly fuzzy. She had enough reality in her life, thank you very much. She turned the TV off and looked around.

Her camera sat on the end table next to the couch. She'd gotten some great shots of the alley during the stakeout a few days ago. She could always develop them now. She even went so far as to carry the camera into her darkroom, but there was no window and, consequently, no relief from the heat that had been building inside all day.

She put the camera back where she'd found it. Next, she brushed the fallen daisy petals into her hand. With a sigh, she threw the entire bouquet of wilted flowers away. She found a brass fan in her dad's old room and plugged it in and turned it on in hers. Yawning, she flopped down on her bed in front of the artificial breeze and sighed.

She was just tired. After all, even night owls got tired.

Turning the radio on low to cover the sounds wafting through her open window, she found herself looking up at her ceiling. She missed Noah.

There, she'd allowed herself to think it. And the sky hadn't fallen and the earth hadn't opened up and the oceans hadn't swelled, as far as she knew. She loved him. There was nothing wrong with missing him. Having him nearby this past week had spoiled her. Having him gone tonight reminded her of how alone she used to feel when he was gone for weeks at a time. She'd let her guard down, and had fallen even deeper in love with him. She prayed she wouldn't be sorry.

Heaving another sigh, she fluffed her pillow and lay back. The music played softly and the fan whirred, stirring warm air that was better than no breeze at all. Her eyes were just beginning to drift closed when her cell phone rang.

There were only three people who had her number. She hoped it was Noah but would have been happy if it was April and wouldn't have minded if it was her new employer, Rosy Sirrine. She checked the caller ID. Rats. It listed the number as unknown. Only someone who was bored and lonely would answer, right?

She slid the phone open and said a tentative, "Hello?"

"Are you in bed?"

"Noah?" she asked more loudly than she'd intended.

"How many other men call you at night and ask if you're in bed?"

She smiled in spite of herself. "I thought you were either a wrong number or a heavy breather. Whose phone are you using?"

"Sam's. Mine's dead and I forgot to pack my charger. Back to the heavy breathing."

Lacey laughed. It sounded slightly provocative and very content.

"Did I ever tell you I like the way you laugh?"

"I don't think so."

"Want to know what else I like?"

She chuckled again. "Oh, no, you don't. I'm not touching that line with a ten-foot pole."

"Spoilsport."

"You'll thank me when you don't need a cold shower." She couldn't help laughing again, though.

"What are you wearing?" he asked.

"If I tell you, that heavy breathing I was worried about is going to be coming from you. How's Texas?"

She could hear him moving around, and imagined him getting comfortable on some bed in a mediocre motel room. He told her about the flight and the lead on the waitress that turned out to be another dead end. They talked about the traffic in Dallas and a dozen other things. She told him about her first day back at The

Hill, and that she'd considered developing the pictures she'd taken these past few days, but hadn't.

"I'd like to watch you do that sometime."

"You want to watch?" she asked.

"I was talking about watching you develop your film, but I'm open to watching you do other things."

"You're a real sport."

This time he laughed.

She stretched sinuously, crossed her ankles and pointed her toes. It was as if that little butterfly tattoo on the top of her foot really fluttered its wings. It set off an entire flurry of sensations up and down her body. She sighed, and smiled, and laughed when he described what he'd had for dinner. The radio played softly and the fan stirred the warm air. She burned up twenty-five of her prepaid minutes. She didn't have it in her to care.

"I wish I was there," he said.

"Put your money where your mouth is, flyboy."

He groaned as if he was thinking where he wanted to put his mouth. "I'll be home tomorrow by three, Michigan time."

"What then?" she asked, surprising herself.

"There's something I want to tell you."

"There's something I want to tell you, too, Noah."

"Good night, Lacey."

"Good night."

Neither of them hung up.

"Noah?" she asked softly.

"Hmm?"

"I'm wearing a white T-shirt you left here a long time ago."

"Anything else?" His voice had warmed at least ten degrees.

She made a humming sound that meant no. She moved her hips a little and imagined him doing the same.

Moaning deep in his throat, he said, "Make that two o'clock Michigan time."

She was smiling when the call ended. She

wasn't going to be sorry she'd let her guard down and opened her heart to Noah. After turning off the lamp, she turned on her side, and was asleep with the radio playing softly and her heart amazingly full.

Chapter Twelve

It was closer to three o'clock than two when Noah finally pulled into his driveway on Tuesday afternoon. He parked between Lacey's car and a little import he didn't recognize. Patting his pocket reassuringly, he took a deep breath, rehearsed his opening line one more time and sauntered on in.

He wasted his entrance on Marsh and Reed and a chunky woman who looked as if she was about to burst into tears as she faced the stony expressions of his older brothers across the kitchen table. Apparently, the temp agency had sent over their first nanny candidate.

Feeling a little sorry for the woman, Noah smiled kindly. "Sorry to interrupt," he said to Marsh and Reed. "Where's Lacey?"

Reed motioned with his head.

As Noah left the room, he heard Marsh say, "Have you had any problems with post-traumatic stress disorder?"

Noah almost turned around. Post-traumatic stress?

He continued toward the front of the house, listening for a clue as to where Lacey might be. He hadn't gone far when he heard her voice. Following that soft croon, he paused in the doorway of the room that was now Joey's nursery.

Lacey sat in the rocking chair in the corner. She held Joey partially upright in one arm. In her other hand she held a colorful storybook.

"...and the dragon came charging out of his cool, dark cave, breathing fire. He roared. And waited for the shrieks of terror he always heard.

"A little boy with auburn hair stood looking at him from a meadow of wildflowers. The dragon roared again. The little boy smiled. And two dimples appeared.

"'Run,' the dragon growled, smoke rising from his nostrils.

"The little boy didn't run. He smiled again and said, 'Would you like to come out and play?'"

Perhaps Lacey felt Noah's presence. Or perhaps she felt his gaze. For whatever reason, she stopped reading and looked up at him.

Warmth bloomed in Noah's chest.

"You're back," she said.

"I'm back."

"Is the interview still going on out there?" she asked.

"I think it's winding down." He made a sound of an explosion and an accompanying gesture with his hands.

"The first one didn't go well, either," she said. "It's possible they're being a tad picky."

He tilted his head. "Feel like taking a walk?"

She closed the book and set it on the corner of the dresser Noah had assembled several days ago. Had it really been less than a week since they'd discovered Joey on their doorstep? Had it really been less than a week since he'd redis-covered Lacey?

Noah reached for his nephew. Settling him at his chest so that he was looking over Noah's left shoulder, he offered a hand to Lacey.

She took it, and rather than interrupting the interview a second time, they went out the front door the family rarely used. This was it, Noah thought as they stepped onto the porch. This was the pinnacle of step three. Up until this point, he had employed the circle, advance and retreat strategy. Patting his pocket where his mother's heirloom ring was waiting, he went over one last time *everything* he'd been re-hearsing. He had so much to tell her about how much he'd missed her these past two-and-a-half years and how much he'd changed since she'd

338 *A Bride Before Dawn*

returned. He wanted her, and he wanted what she'd always wanted.

They started along the lane. They went west this time, away from the two-track that led to the meadow. He patted the pocket of his jeans again. When he finally spoke, it was to ask a question. "If you could go back and do things differently, would you?"

She looked up at him in the dappled shade on the winding path. Joey was content in Noah's arms, his eyes bright as he watched the world behind them.

"You mean do something the easy way?" she asked. "Who, me? Us?"

He smiled, one hand on Joey's back. "Do you remember the first night Joey was here? I pounded on your door and threatened to break it down if you didn't let me in."

"I vaguely remember that," she said drolly.

"I wanted him to be ours."

Lacey turned her head so fast she nearly gave herself whiplash. Had she heard correctly?

she wondered. "But I thought you didn't want children."

"That's what I thought, too."

Lacey's heart was racing, her thoughts spinning. Noah had always looked dangerous around the edges, but he'd never looked as dangerous as he looked this afternoon, his hair freshly cut, his face clean-shaven, the truth bare in his golden-brown eyes.

The birds were busy tending their nests in the branches overhead. To Lacey's ears, their melody sounded like a song played on the piano with one finger. Duh-duh-duh-da.

"You look surprised," he said. "I don't blame you. It surprised me, too. I've been rehearsing this for hours and I haven't said any of this the way I'd planned."

They'd stopped walking and now stood in the dappled shade of an enormous weeping-willow tree. Patting Joey's back, he said, "When you were reading that story to him a few minutes ago, all I could think was how amazing it's going to be when it's our baby in your arms."

Lacey felt something under her sandal. She wouldn't have been surprised if it had been her lower jaw. Actually, it was a small blue sock. She bent down automatically. Picking it up gave her something to do with her hands and something to look at besides the naked truth in Noah's eyes.

"Noah, there's something you should know."

"What is it?" he asked, pointing to the baby bootee in her hand. Evidently noticing her stricken look, he said, "Lacey, what's wrong?"

She handed him the little sock. Turning it over in his hand, he gazed back toward the house and said, "This was where she waited."

She could hear her heart beating in her ears. It wasn't easy to hear anything else. "This was where who waited?" she asked.

"Joey's mother."

The wispy willow branches arched to the ground here, brushing the grass in the slight breeze. The tree stood between them and the house. Through the fronds, Lacey could see all the way to the front porch.

"Are you saying this is Joey's sock?" she asked.

Noah nodded. "He was wearing the other one when we found him. This one was missing. She must have waited here with him. It probably slipped off his foot before she worked up the courage to creep out of her hiding place. I saw her. When I was flying over. I saw a woman hurrying across the front lawn. After she left him on the front porch, she probably hid here until she knew Joey was safely inside."

Lacey's heart was still pounding with the knowledge that Noah wanted children. A car drove by. It was the woman Marsh and Reed had interviewed leaving in her little import.

"I've gotten off the subject." He smiled at her. When she failed to smile back, he said, "What is it?"

She shook her head. She couldn't have found

her voice right then if her life had depended on it.

"I didn't plan to do this with Joey along," he said. "But now I think maybe it's fitting that he's here for this. After all, his arrival is what finally opened my eyes."

He felt his pocket again.

Unable to speak, she shook her head and backed up a step.

"Lacey, what's wrong? What the hell is it? You're scaring me."

Noah hadn't meant to speak so loudly. Too late he saw Joey's little lip quiver. The baby started to cry. Noah felt like a goddamn monster. "I didn't mean to frighten you, buddy."

Jiggling the baby, he tried to reach Lacey, too. He didn't know what was going on. What had he said? What had he done wrong? Her face had paled. And her eyes, those forget-me-not blue eyes, were swimming with tears.

She took another step back. Away from him. At first he didn't understand what she was doing. She hiked her shirt up. For a second there he got a little sidetracked by the sight of bare skin. She hitched her shirt a little higher and unbuttoned her jeans.

"What are you doing?" he asked.

Her zipper went down. And then, with both hands, she slung her jeans open to reveal her belly.

His first thought was—

He forgot his first thought. For the first time he noticed two scars on her stomach. "What happened?" he said.

Joey was wailing and Lacey was shaking her head and backing up. "I can't have your babies, Noah."

She spun around and hurried toward the house.

"Lacey, come back."

Joey cried harder. And Lacey started running. Noah didn't know what the hell to do about either one of them. One thing he did know. He had to calm down.

As he rocked Joey to and fro, the woman he loved ran to the house. She went in the front door that not even company used. Less than a minute later she went out the back. Still running, she got in her car. And then she drove away.

Okay. This was a new low, even for Noah. He'd raised a lot of hell in his life, and he'd made people pull their hair out. He'd brought more than one woman to tears, teachers mostly. He hadn't spent a lot of time with kids, but he might have made one or two of them cry, too. He'd never made a woman and a baby cry at the same time.

He parked in the alley by Bell's Tavern twenty minutes after Lacey had fled. He'd tried calling her. She hadn't answered. Her car was here, but that didn't mean she was home.

He'd shown the baby sock to Marsh and Reed, and briefly explained where Lacey had found it. Reed had taken Joey and Marsh took the sock.

Reed told him that Lacey had run out of the house, crying. "I don't know what's going on," he said. "But go after her."

"We've got things covered here," Marsh had insisted. "Go."

It was the best advice his brothers had ever given him. Now that he was here, the adrenaline rush that had gotten him this far lost pressure like air through a leaky valve.

He threw the shifting lever into Park, set the brake and got out. He paced back and forth in front of the barrel of petunias. He wasn't sure where he'd gone wrong, and while he didn't understand what had precipitated Lacey's reaction, the image of her scars and the echo of her voice as she'd said, "I can't have your babies, Noah," was embedded in his brain. Once his thoughts were in a semblance of order, he took the steps two at a time and knocked on her door.

Lacey was in her bedroom when she heard the pounding. She'd splashed her face with cool water, fixed her mascara and tied her hair up for work at The Hill. She wasn't surprised that Noah had come looking for her. As far as explanations went, hers left a lot to be desired. She'd definitely stuck to the facts. Or one fact. She couldn't have Noah's babies.

For the second time in less than a week, the pounding on her door got louder. "It's me, Lacey. Open the door."

Noah.

She was on her way across the small living room when the pounding got harder and his voice louder. "I'm not leaving until we've talked. If you don't open up, I'll break the door down."

She turned the dead bolt and stepped back.

The door swung in. For just a moment, neither she nor Noah moved.

Her breath caught at the sight of him. His jeans were faded, his legs long, his chest broad, his breathing a little ragged. His eyes were narrowed, his jaw set. Short hair or not, he had *bad boy* written all over him.

"Either come in or go out," she said. "You're letting in flies."

He came in. And he closed the door. He took a few steps, stopped. Heaving a great sigh, he said, "Tell me about those scars."

She didn't ask him to sit down. He couldn't have sat, and neither could she. Heaving a sigh, too, she said, "Six-and-a-half months ago, I woke up with a mild ache in my side. No big deal, right? I thought I was just ovulating, or something I'd eaten didn't agree with me. I took some aspirin and went to my temp job. By midnight, I couldn't take the pain. I went to the E.R. Emergency rooms are busy places in large cities in the middle of the night. Six hours later, I was in surgery."

"What was wrong?" he asked.

"It was just my appendix. Ninety-nine-point-nine percent of the time, appendectomies are routine. In, out, patients are good to go. You know me. I don't do anything the easy way. There was an infection. To make a long story short, I lived. But the internal scarring damaged my fallopian tubes, the right one more than the left. They actually took a photograph of my insides. It wasn't a pretty picture."

She went to the table and picked up a sheet of paper, with line after line of dollar amounts. "This is a little souvenir of my vacation in the hospital. It's the reason I came back to Orchard Hill. I have to sell the tavern to pay the hospital back for saving my life."

Noah had eased closer during her little speech. With every step he took, she raised her eyes a little more, never wavering from his gaze. "God, Lace. You could have died."

"I didn't. The only thing that died was my dream of having kids. Just because I can't doesn't mean you can't."

"What are you talking about?"

"You want them, Noah. You should have them. It would be a crying shame not to pass on all those incredible genes. So this is it. It's been fun."

Her voice shook a little, but not too badly.

"It has been fun," he said. The edge in his voice was sharp enough to cut steel.

Noah couldn't decide if he should wrap his arms around Lacey or throttle her. In the end, he snatched the sheet of paper from her hand, scanned it and stuffed it in his back pocket. "The goddamn fun isn't over yet," he said, on his way to the door. "Don't even think about leaving town because I will hunt you down."

"*You're* mad at *me?*"

He sucked in a breath and spun around. The floor shook beneath his feet as he stomped back to her. He slid his fingers into her hair and covered her mouth with his. He took her gasp of surprise into his own mouth.

The kiss was neither punishing nor particularly sensual. It was a brand. It was an exclamation point. It lasted only a matter of seconds, but it wasn't the end of anything.

"I'm mad at you because I love you."

As Noah left Lacey's apartment, he didn't

know for sure where he was going. He didn't have a plan. He wished to hell he did. This was no time to resort to flying by the seat of his pants. What else could he do?

One thing was certain. He would be back, and by God she had better get used to the idea, because after he figured this one out, he wasn't leaving again.

Chapter Thirteen

Waitress uniforms weren't required at The Hill. Rosy asked only that her employees show up for work on time and were clean, courteous and pleasant to her customers and each other. The busboys wore full aprons and the waitresses short white ones with pockets large enough to hold an order book, pen and tips.

At the end of Lacey's shift on her second night, only one customer remained. And he was no ordinary customer.

Noah had been holding up the end of the

counter for the better part of an hour. He'd ordered a Coke, but as far as she could tell, the ice had melted and he hadn't taken so much as a sip. He was too busy stalking her with his eyes.

The other waitress was putting up chairs in the back. All Lacey had left to do was wipe down the counter. As she wrung out her cloth, she happened to glance at Rosy, who was counting money at the cash register. "Choose your battles, dearie," the older woman said.

Along with a secretive past and an uncanny habit of spouting pearls of wisdom at the precise moment they were needed, Rosy Sirrine possessed the rare ability to raise one eyebrow independently of the other. She demonstrated that move for Lacey while casting a pointed look at Noah, then resumed counting.

There was no sense wondering how the woman could have known. "Noah," Lacey finally said when he lifted his elbows from the marred Formica surface, indicating that she should clean up around him. "We're closed. You shouldn't be here."

He drank his entire glass of watered-down Coke without saying a word. But he didn't leave.

"I'll finish up, Lacey," Rosy said. "Go ahead and go."

She untied her apron and left it on the counter. Noah slid off the stool. He fell into step beside her, held the door for her, then clamped his fingers around her wrist.

"What are you doing?" she asked.

"I'm giving you a ride home." It was the first words he'd spoken since ordering that Coke.

Lacey stood looking at him on the sidewalk in front of The Hill.

There were only a few people on the sidewalk. If Lacey had chosen to scream, someone would have come to her rescue. She wouldn't scream. She wasn't the least bit afraid. She was curious and a tad nervous, but she knew Noah wouldn't hurt her.

He had something to say. He'd told her he

loved her and that he wished Joey were theirs. The least she could do was listen. So she let him lead her to his passenger-side door. When he opened it, she got in.

Absently rubbing the wrist he'd just unhanded, she buckled her seat belt and turned the tables on him, her gaze now stalking him. He caught every green light. It would be cruel of her to say this was his lucky day. It would also be a lie.

He pulled into the alley and parked next to her borrowed car. She got out. And he did, too.

"Upstairs," he said.

"Do not order me around." She raised her fighter's chin and started up the newly painted steps.

Noah followed her up the stairs. She unlocked her door, opened it and went in. He closed it quietly. She dropped her purse on the coffee table and raised her eyes to his.

"Okay," he said, as if a minute had elapsed since she'd told him about her surgery, instead of six hours. "Your appendix ruptured, and there was an infection and some scarring. What else did your doctor say?"

She made a sound of impatience then set about opening windows. She hadn't intended to end up in her bedroom, but it was too late now because he'd followed her there. He turned on a fan, rested his rear end on the edge of her dresser and settled in.

She looked beyond him at her reflection in the mirror. As usual, her hair had defied the metal clasp. Dark tendrils had escaped, framing her face and falling over the collar of her ivory-colored blouse.

"You want to know what my doctor said?" she parroted.

He nodded and crossed his ankles and arms.

Her long-suffering sighs didn't seem to faze him.

"My doctor said my appendix had ruptured several hours before my surgery began. There was an infection."

"And the infection caused internal scarring," he prodded. "How much scarring?"

She folded her arms, too. "You want a percentage?" she asked.

"Actually, I do."

"I don't know what percentage of my innards are scarred, all right? But I can tell you that my fallopian tubes were damaged, the right one more than the left."

"How much more?" he asked.

"Noah, what in the world? My doctor told me there is a ninety-two-percent chance I'll never conceive."

The fan whirred and the barest hint of a breeze jostled the blinds at her window. He uncrossed his ankles, unfolded his arms and stood up. "Just so there's no confusion," he said, moving stealthily toward her, "I would have done this if you'd told me the number was a hundred percent."

"You would have done what?" she asked.

Oh, she talked tough, but she heard the little

telltale hitch in her own breathing, and she felt the flutter of hope in her chest. He took another step toward her. He reached into his pocket, and held his hand out to her.

"Would you marry me, Lacey?"

She couldn't believe her ears or her eyes. She was pretty sure Noah had just proposed. If she could have looked into his eyes, she would have known whether or not she'd heard right, but she couldn't take her gaze off the ring he held delicately between his thumb and one finger.

Her hands went to her cheeks before she could stop them. She didn't even try to check her tears. The ring, made of gold, was caught in the lamplight. On the dainty side, it contained a swirl of what looked like diamonds, sapphires, rubies and an aqua-colored stone she couldn't identify.

She finally looked up at Noah. The glint in his eyes was more inspiring than the ring.

"But, Noah, I can't give you children."

"Why do you always have to look on the negative side?"

Her chin came up a notch. "I'm being realist—"

"There's a ninety-two-percent chance you'll have trouble conceiving. I did the math. There's a good chance you will."

"You call eight percent good?"

He smiled, and eased a little closer, the ring still in his outstretched hand. "Honey, eight goes into a hundred, what, twelve-and-a-half times? That means we'll have to make love twelve times more than normal. I don't know about you, but I'm up for the challenge."

The scathing look she gave him would have brought some men to their knees. It invigorated Noah.

Lacey almost couldn't help smiling. The man was inspiring, no doubt about it. She held up one hand. "All challenges aside, Noah, there's a chance, a good chance, I won't conceive. You want children. You deserve them. I won't blame you if you walk out the door right now and find somebody who can give you better odds."

She held her breath, terrified that he might do just that.

"We'll try," he said. "We'll try hard. And if that doesn't work, we'll see a specialist. And if that doesn't work, we'll adopt, or spoil our nieces and nephews rotten. We'll be a family of two or three or ten. As long as I have you, I'll be happy."

A tear ran down her face.

Wiping it away with the pad of his thumb, he said, "I want to hear you say it."

She started. "Say what?"

"That you'll marry me."

A smile bloomed on her lips. Just below it a butterfly lit at the little hollow at the base of her throat. Below that, a thousand wings fluttered. She tipped her head to one side and studied this man who was as stubborn as she was, as wild as she was, as crazy as she was. "Fine, I'll marry you. But don't say I didn't warn you."

She was about to throw herself into his arms. Luckily one of them had the sense to remember the ring. He took her left hand and slid the ring on her finger. She had to help him get it past her knuckle. It fit her as if it was made for her, the way the glass slipper fit Cinderella in the fairy tale.

"This isn't just any ring," Noah said. "My dad gave it to my mother when he proposed. His father gave it to his bride before that. It comes down through a long line of tenacious, determined people—people with deep roots and long memories."

She sniffled. Admiring the colors in the stones, she said, "Do you think you could kiss me now?"

His arms came around her. In that moment before his lips touched hers, he said, "I can do a hell of a lot better than that."

Her arms went around him, too, and she lifted her face to his. The thing about Noah was that he kissed with everything he had. He poured everything into it, his heart, his soul, and he had a lot of both.

She drew her arms tight around him, holding him to her, and her to him. Slowly, her hands glided up to his shoulders, and back down again. She loved his back, loved the corded muscles and sinew, loved his narrow hips and rear end. Her hands went there, squeezing.

Something crinkled in his pocket. She reached in like a street urchin and brought out a sheet of paper.

She gave herself up to his kiss for another full minute. She moaned into his mouth, and sighed at his touch. His fingers went to the buttons on her shirt.

She spun around, fitting her back to his front. Never one to pass up any opportunity, he covered her breasts with his hands. He seemed to know instinctively how much pressure to exert, squeezing without hurting her, kneading until she arched her back and brought one hand to the nape of his neck.

She opened her eyes, and once again noticed the piece of paper in her hand. She unfolded it, and scanned it. It was the itemized bill from the hospital in Chicago. She'd gone over it dozens of times. The *PAID IN FULL* scrawled across the columns was new.

"What's this?" she asked.

He groaned at being interrupted in the middle of kissing her neck. "Oh, that."

Something about those two words breached the haze of her desire. "Why does it say *paid in full?*"

"Because I wired the money to the hospital a few hours ago."

"You what?" She turned around. And looked him square in the face. "How?"

"Modern technology."

That wasn't what she was asking. "This was for tens of thousands of dollars. How could you have paid it off? Even if you sold your truck, you wouldn't—"

Her breath caught. There was only one thing he could have sold for this much money.

"Oh, Noah, you didn't sell your airplane."

Noah took a deep, fortifying breath. He couldn't do anything about what was happening below his waist, but he attempted to clear his mind by blinking his eyes.

"I thought maybe we could talk about this later—" He made a little jerking gesture toward the bed with his shoulder. "But obviously you want to talk about it now."

A circle of pink appeared on her cheeks. He knew what it meant. She was miffed.

"Look, I had three offers before I took her for a test flight. I accepted the best one. There will be other planes."

"How could you? This was my responsibility. I had every intention of paying this off as soon as the tavern sells. Someone's interested in it, by the way."

"Fine," he said, adopting her favorite word and stance. "When it sells, you can buy us that house with a picket fence you've always wanted."

"You would accept that? You would live in a house I bought? You wouldn't have a problem knowing you were a kept man?"

He supposed he shouldn't have grinned, but he couldn't help it. "As long as you're the woman keeping me, oh, yeah, I'd be as happy as a clam."

It must have been the right thing to say, because she tipped her head and gave her shoulders a little shrug. "I guess we would be even then, wouldn't we?" she asked.

Darkness had fallen. The only sound in the room was the whir of the fan behind them and a moth beating its wings incessantly against the screen in its never-ending quest for the light. Noah had never understood such a quest better than right now.

"Are you done talking?" he asked.

She shrugged again, then stepped back into

his arms. He curled his body around her, and said, "Can I get that in writing?"

She moaned deep in her throat. "Get what in writing? That we're done talking?"

"No, that you'll marry me—the sooner the better."

"Why don't we just elope so I can't change my mind?"

He smiled. "That's a great idea."

She opened her eyes wide. "I was being sarcastic."

"I know. You sound like a wife already. Let's do it. Let's elope."

"Now?"

He nodded.

"But how? Who would marry us at this time on a Tuesday night?"

Their gazes met, held. They had the same idea at the same time. "The judge," they said in unison.

She chortled. "Can you imagine what Ivan the Terrible will say if we wake him up?"

Imagine it? Noah had been waiting ten years for an opportunity like this. "Come on." He took her hand.

"Wait." She looked down at her mussed shirt and faded jeans. "I'm only going to get married once, Noah Sullivan. Give me ten minutes to change my clothes and fix my hair."

"I'll give you ten minutes if you'll give me one minute to do this."

He tipped her face up and kissed her.

Lacey gave herself up to the moment, a moment that lasted far longer than a minute. Somewhere, somehow, while his lips melded with hers, and his breath became her breath, she heard a clock strike midnight. Breathless with wonder after the kiss ended, she fairly floated to the closet and brought out the dress she would wear to become Noah's bride.

The houses on Jefferson Street were some of the oldest and largest in all of Orchard Hill.

Noah parked at the curb and peered at the dark windows of his uncle's intimidating mansion.

He ran around and opened the door for his bride. He'd waited longer than ten minutes for Lacey to get ready, but when she'd emerged from her bedroom, a vision in that aqua cloud of a dress, her face serene, her eyes shining with anticipation and happiness, it was worth every minute he'd waited.

Hand in hand, they ran up the sidewalk. They couldn't believe they were doing this. He pressed the doorbell. From somewhere on the second floor, a yappy dog started barking. Noah stood holding Lacey's hand, fireflies flitting above the rosebushes on either side of the front door. When the barking stopped and no one came, he pressed the doorbell again.

Just as he was about to ring the bell the third time, the foyer light came on. "Who is it?" a grumpy voice asked.

"Why, it's Noah, dear." Noah's plump, gray-haired great-aunt opened the door and blinked in the bright light, a little gray dog on one arm.

"What are you doing here?" the judge groused, blinking owlishly, too.

"We'd like to get married," Noah said.

"Come to the courthouse in the morning." He started to slam the door, only to have his efforts thwarted by his wife.

"Don't you kids mind his fe-fi-fo-fumming. Come in. This is so romantic. Isn't this romantic, Ivan, dear?"

"What's romantic about being awakened out of the best sleep I've had in weeks?" He peered up at Noah, his comb-over sticking out, his eyes watery behind his smudged wire-rimmed glasses. He gave his great-nephew a look that usually made even the toughest, thick-skinned people fidget. Tonight, Noah held the judge's gaze unwaveringly. In that moment, something passed between them. And even though the judge heaved a condescending sigh, Noah realized it covered genuine affection. "I guess

I'm awake now," the old man said. "I might as well make an honest man out of you. Maude, bring me my—"

She'd already thought of that, and came bustling back into the room before he'd finished the command. In her hands were a worn leather-bound book and two legal-looking documents, her satiny robe and fluffy dog fluttering behind her.

"I don't remember the last time some young couple woke us up to marry them. There's just a dab of paperwork to fill out so it's all nice and legal," she said, beaming up at Noah and Lacey. "By the way, I'm Aunt Maude."

Lacey smiled so warmly even Ivan noticed.

"Why, aren't you a pretty little thing," Maude exclaimed, wetting the tip of her pen with her tongue.

She asked them pertinent questions, and filled in the blanks with their answers. And then the judge led them to the living room.

He stood with his back to the stone fireplace. And Noah took Lacey's hand.

There was no violin music, no candlelight, no flowers, no church filled with guests, or bridesmaids in taffeta and pearls. Lacey had never wanted any of those things. All she'd ever wanted was the love of the man holding her hand.

And Noah did love her. She believed it with her whole heart. She loved him, too, just as much.

As she stood waiting for the civil ceremony to begin, she thought she heard her father's voice whisper, "Didn't I tell you you'd find the hidden treasure?"

Feeling almost as light as the air she breathed, she smiled and whispered back, "Thanks, Dad."

The judge cleared his throat and began. He asked the *Do you*'s and said the *Repeat after me*'s. The ceremony lasted five minutes at the most. Noah and Lacey had no wedding rings to exchange. They had something greater. They exchanged promises to love, honor and cherish each other as long as they both lived.

"By the power vested in me," the judge said, "by God and the State of Michigan, I now pronounce you husband and wife."

Great-Aunt Maude sniffled. When the judge forgot the best part, she whispered, "You may kiss your bride."

Noah eased his face closer to Lacey's. And he kissed his wife for the very first time. Lacey closed her eyes and kissed her husband, too.

She forgot her camera, but Great-Aunt Maude snapped several pictures before they left. Already Lacey knew what she would write at the top when she put them in her scrapbook.

A Bride & Her Groom Before Dawn.

And just like that, the beginning of their brand-new beginning began.

Epilogue

Three days before Christmas...

Noah turned up his wool collar against the morning chill and watched as a few more guests arrived for this morning's traditional wedding ceremony. Well, he thought, sliding a hand into the pocket of his full-length black coat, this was as traditional as he and Lacey could be.

Having another wedding ceremony with his closest friends and family in attendance had been Noah's idea. Having it outdoors on a cold winter morning beneath an arbor decorated with pine boughs and holly at the orchard had been Lacey's.

But he was getting ahead of himself.

The notion to have a second ceremony had occurred to him in the middle of the night a week ago. By the time Lacey had awakened beside him at dawn's early light, he'd had an entire night to revel in the wonder that he and Lacey were going to have a baby—two, actually.

But of course there would be two! Noah's three-step plan had had a mind of its own from the start. Why would he have thought that had changed? He loved the way everything had worked out. His genes and Lacey's had found one another in a petri dish. Now, nine weeks later they were snug as two bugs in a rug inside their mother's uterus. Noah had lain awake in awe the entire night following their first ultrasound appointment.

"Our kids are going to want to know our story," he'd whispered into Lacey's ear.

She'd hummed an agreeable sound.

"We have to make sure it's a good story," he'd insisted.

"Stories don't get much better than ours," she'd answered on a sigh.

"I want to show them a photo album of our wedding and all our guests," he'd said.

That brought her the rest of the way awake. "You want us to get married again?"

"I thought you'd never ask!" He'd placed his hand over her belly, only now just starting to round. And although he couldn't feel their children, he and Lacey both believed their babies felt the love radiating from their daddy's hand. Within minutes, the plans were made, their closest family and friends were called, and here they were, a week later, about to exchange their vows one more time.

Joey, nine months old now, babbled loudly from his mother's arms behind Noah. It appeared that Charlotte, Noah's niece and Riley and Madeline's three-month-old daughter, was going to sleep through the outdoor ceremony of her *favorite* aunt and uncle. Noah had a couple of brothers and two sisters-in-law who would have disputed that particular designation. After all, the only thing the Sullivan brothers enjoyed more than loving their wives was claiming bragging rights to uncle-ship. It never ceased to amaze Noah when he thought about the fact that all four of the Sullivans—Madeline, Reed, Marsh and Noah—had married the same year.

As if they'd read his mind, Reed and Marsh suddenly appeared on either side of Noah. "The judge is ready," Marsh said.

"Everybody's here," Reed added.

They each clapped him on a shoulder, and the girl Noah had first glimpsed climbing out the window above the tavern last June raised her violin to her shoulder. And the beautiful undulating notes of "Joy to the World" swirled like love itself to the ears of each wedding guest gathered in the meadow where Noah had written *LACEY + NOAH* six months ago.

Even Joey quieted. All eyes turned to the

vision in a flowing velvet cape stepping into view from inside the cider house nearby.

Lacey took a moment to let her gaze rest on the glowing faces of her best friends, and her sisters-in-law and brothers-in-law. They all stood beaming back at her, smiles on their faces. Even the judge wore a warm glow this morning.

What a morning! Something had happened in the atmosphere overnight, and with the rising of the sun, it was as if the universe was telling her this morning was a gift for her and Noah. There was a dusting of snow on the ground and on everything—every roof and every branch of every tree—was frost so sparkling and white it was almost too much beauty to take in with only one's eyes. It was as if it needed to be felt, too, in order to be fully appreciated. It reminded her of the love she saw as her gaze met Noah's.

She started down the stone steps of the cider house as the lovely strains of that single violin continued. She had no one to escort her to the arbor where Noah and the judge waited, and yet she had no fear of tripping. Later everyone would tell her she appeared to float down the steps and along the curving pathway. But Lacey knew she wasn't floating, for she felt the firm foundation of the earth beneath her every step.

Noah had never looked more handsome than he did at that moment when he reached out his hand, and cradled her cold fingers in his warm palm. April swooped forward and lowered the velvety hood of Lacey's cape. The music ended. And the judge began.

"Dearly beloved, we are gathered here this morning to once again join these two in marriage…"

One of the babies started crying while Lacey and Noah were saying their vows. By the time Lacey and Noah both said, "I do," the babies weren't the only ones sniffling.

Lacey's and Noah's eyes remained dry. A

slight breeze wafted across the meadow, and suddenly the air was filled with bits of frost glittering like starlight in the light of day.

Noah kissed his bride, even though they'd been officially married for six months. Never let it be said that a Sullivan didn't take every advantage handed to him.

What a Christmas, she thought, slightly dizzy with happiness as she and Noah faced their family. As everyone hugged everyone else and backs were patted and babies jiggled, it felt to Lacey as if she'd been in this exact moment before. She couldn't explain it, but with Noah at her side and their children growing within her, and all these people to love and be loved, it already felt like Christmas.

As Lacey held out her hands to Joey, and Noah took Madeline's little girl and Riley's baby in his arms, and all the family gathered around them, they all knew that Christmas wasn't just a day. Christmas was the belief, the innocent trust in a misunderstood universe that something joyful was coming. It had nothing to do with what was material, and everything to do with what wasn't.

* * * * *